TREASURE AT
BLUE HERON LAKE

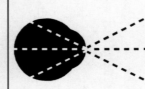

TREASURE AT BLUE HERON LAKE

A ROMANCE MYSTERY

SUSAN PAGE DAVIS AND MEGAN ELAINE DAVIS

THORNDIKE PRESS

A part of Gale, Cengage Learning

GALE
CENGAGE Learning™

Detroit • New York • San Francisco • New Haven, Conn • Waterville, Maine • London

GALE
CENGAGE Learning™

© 2008 by Susan Page Davis and Megan Elaine Davis.
Scripture taken from the HOLY BIBLE, NEW INTERANTIONAL VERSION®, NIV®. Copyright © 1973, 1978, 1984 by International Bible Society. Used by permission of Zondervan. All rights reserved.
Thorndike Press, a part of Gale, Cengage Learning.

LIBRARY OF CONGRESS CATALOGING-IN-PUBLICATION DATA

Davis, Susan Page.
  Treasure at Blue Heron Lake : a romance mystery / by Susan Page Davis and Megan Elaine Davis. — Large print ed.
    p. cm. — (Mainely mysteries ; bk. 2) (Thorndike Press large print Christian mystery)
  ISBN-13: 978-1-4104-3300-8
  ISBN-10: 1-4104-3300-5
  1. Large type books. I. Davis, Megan Elaine. II. Title.
PS3604.A976T74 2011
813'.6—dc22   2010040637

Published in 2011 by arrangement with Barbour Publishing, Inc.

Printed in Mexico
1 2 3 4 5 6 7 15 14 13 12 11

Megan:
For my fiancé, John-Mark, who dreams and believes, and whose laugh is contagious. Thank you for caring about my writing. Thank you for knowing I could do it. Love, your Meg.

Susan:
For my sweet little granddaughter Naomi, whom I look forward to getting to know. Love, Grammy.

ACKNOWLEDGMENTS

Our thanks to retired Maine state trooper Paul Stewart for pointers on police procedure. Thanks also to our critique partners, Darlene, Lynette, and Lisa, and to Jim, loving husband and dear daddy, our "first reader."

1

> For where your treasure is, there your
> heart will be also.
>
> MATTHEW 6:21 NIV

A bull moose stepped out of the woods a hundred feet ahead of Nate Holman's SUV, stopping in the gravel road and staring at the vehicle. Emily caught her breath. Nate braked, throwing gravel up from beneath the tires of his eight-year-old vehicle, and came to a halt five yards from the animal. The moose watched them with huge, placid eyes then ambled across the road and into the woods, tipping his head so his antlers didn't scrape the trees.

"You okay?" Nate asked.

"Yeah." Emily brushed the hair out of her eyes. "That was a big one."

"I wouldn't want to see him any closer."

Emily's pulse slowed as they continued down the road and came in sight of the imposing, three-story Lakeview Lodge. She was ready for a quiet weekend with Nate and his friend.

The building wore its age well. It was roomy but homelike, with seasoned cedar shingle siding and holiday swags over each doorway. To Emily, the lodge's late-nineteenth-century architecture offered the promise of a fascinating history.

Still, it was hard to imagine well-heeled sportsmen coming to such a plain resort, and she'd been forewarned that the plumbing was so old it was almost primitive. She supposed that if someone wanted to hunt moose or launch a snowmobile trip into Canada, there was no better place than this rustic lodge in Baxter, Maine.

"Like it?" Nate asked.

"Love it. Thanks for bringing me here."

He got out and came around to open her door for her then raised the rear door of his SUV to retrieve their overnight bags.

Emily was glad to be going anywhere with Nate Holman. She'd loved him for years, and she was confident their relationship would soon take a turn for the permanent. Thinking about it sent a zing of anticipation through her as she watched him. In his down parka and L.L.Bean boots, he was handsome enough to turn heads at the

Bangor mall. Just wait until he started wearing the uniform of the Penobscot County Sheriff's Department in a few months.

"You should get plenty of information for your article." Nate handed her the camera bag and closed the back of the SUV.

"I hope to profile every business in Baxter this winter. This article has to be good enough to convince Felicia to let me continue the series." Her editor at the twice-weekly *Baxter Journal* wasn't so sure business stories would draw enough reader interest, but Emily was determined to prove her wrong.

"I think that's great." Nate walked beside her up the steps. "Jeff will be easy to interview, I'm sure."

She grinned. "Yes, as I recall, he was on the debate team in high school."

As they entered the front door of the lodge, the owner strode from his office.

"Nate! I'm so glad you two could come." He shook Nate's hand, smiling broadly. "And you're Emily. It's been a long time."

"It sure has."

Jeff Lewis turned to study her, and she returned the scrutiny. He wore his dark, curly hair short, and his vivid green eyes expressed confidence. Jeff graduated from Aswontee High School a year ahead of Emily and Nate, she remembered. He had played basketball and baseball on the school teams and was a good student, well liked by both boys and girls. She knew that in recent years, while she was living in Connecticut, Jeff and Nate had become close friends. Now that she was back in Baxter, she was glad to get to know the people Nate cared about.

"Nice to have you here," Jeff said. "So, you work for the *Journal.* I've seen your stories."

"Yes." Emily smiled. "It's odd to be working in the same office my parents ran when I was a kid. Thanks for letting me do the article."

"Hey, I can use the publicity," Jeff said. "Of course, most of my guests come from farther away, but it's good to maintain a presence in the community."

"I'm not sure I've ever been inside this building." She looked around as they stepped into the large living area that took the place of a hotel's lobby.

"I'll warn you, we're very casual. And I'll be closing the lodge soon for remodeling."

"Remodeling?" Nate asked. "It's perfect the way it is."

Jeff laughed and led them to the stairway. "Hardly. This place hasn't been updated since my grandfather bought it in the 1930s. Our repeat guests love it and tolerate the ancient plumbing. But it's time."

He guided them along a narrow hallway on the second floor and showed them two rooms. Emily's, decorated with Maine-made pine furniture and pink and green accents, overlooked Blue Heron Lake. Nate's room across the hall had a masculine red plaid color scheme and a view of the softwood forest behind the lodge.

"It's beautiful," Emily said.

"Thanks. You're my only guests tonight, since it's Thanksgiving, but I have several hunting parties coming in tomorrow. Emily, you can have this bathroom, and Nate can use the one down the hall. That's one reason we're remodeling. Guests nowadays expect a private bathroom. Seventy-five or eighty years ago, that wasn't so important."

"How many bathrooms are you adding?" Nate asked.

Jeff grimaced. "Ten. But that's not the thing that prodded me to make changes. Thanks to the insurance company, we'll be closed for about three months this winter."

"Three months?" Emily eyed the outdated bathroom fixtures. The claw-footed iron bathtub was rather charming.

"Yeah, the insurance agent told me they

won't renew my policy unless I have the wiring completely redone. You can understand why."

Nate reached to pull the chain on the overhead light in the bathroom. "You mean things like this?"

"Exactly." Jeff shrugged. "I've been saving up and planning to do this, but not quite so soon. I've known for years that I'd have to. The original wiring is minimal. One light per room, and outlets are almost non-existent."

"How old is this place, anyway?" Emily asked.

"It was built in the 1890s as the bunkhouse for a lumber company. They didn't have electricity in here then, though. That was first done in the '30s, when Grandpa bought it and turned it into a guest lodge. My dad had the kitchen rewired about ten years ago, but he couldn't afford to do the rest, so we kept our primitive ambiance. But now . . . well, I've got to bite the bullet, so I got financing. We're starting right after Christmas." Jeff glanced at his watch. "Hey, it's almost dinnertime. Why don't you two get settled and join me downstairs?"

Emily took a few minutes to brush her hair and hang up the outfit she'd brought for the next day. Nate had told her that dinner would be Maine woods casual, so she didn't change out of her jeans and fisherman's sweater. When she found her way down the stairs into the living area, she could hear the men's voices coming from the adjacent dining room, and she stepped into the doorway.

"Hi, Emily!" Jeff said. He and Nate both stood, and she joined them at a window table. Outside she could see beyond a wide porch to the vast lake, darkened by twilight.

"I gave the staff the day off," Jeff said, "but the cook fixed most of our dinner last night. All I did was put it in the oven, so if it's good, the compliments go to Lucille."

"Can I help you?" Emily asked.

"Well, sure. Thanks."

She followed him into the big, high-ceilinged room. Yes, this would be the place to cook for a camp full of lumberjacks. Everything was large — worktable, counter, pans, and sink. The appliances were modern restaurant style, no doubt thanks to Jeff's father's changes a decade ago.

"I'll bring the meat loaf and rolls. Can you get the potatoes and salad?" Jeff asked.

"What, no leftover turkey?" Nate grinned as they set the dishes on the table in the dining room.

"No, I went to Bangor and had a big dinner this noon with my sister's family," Jeff said. "I figured you'd done the same with yours."

"Pretty much," Nate agreed. "My mom fixed her usual huge Thanksgiving dinner, and the pastor invited several people from church who didn't have other holiday plans to join us."

"That's right, your mother lives in the parsonage now," Jeff said. "When did she remarry?"

"In September."

"She's very happy," Emily said.

Jeff eyed Nate. "How do you like having a stepfather?"

"Oh, he's great. But I'm rattling around in the old house alone now." Nate glanced at Emily, and for no good reason, she felt her cheeks flush.

Well, maybe there is a good reason, she thought. *It's no secret that I love him madly. The logical projection is that he won't be living alone forever.*

She reached for her water glass and took a sip, but it did nothing to cool the fire in her cheeks.

"Well, let's ask the blessing," Jeff said with a knowing smile.

After dinner, he gave them a more complete tour of the old lodge, explaining his

16

plans for the renovations. Emily jotted notes as they looked into the other guest rooms and staff quarters.

"So far all I've done is get estimates," Jeff said, "but the rewiring will start soon. I just hope I don't ruin the flavor of the place by making changes."

"It's going to be even better," Nate assured him. "Sounds like you're making every effort to keep the lumber camp feel but add modern conveniences."

"I'd like to take pictures tomorrow, when the light is better," Emily said.

"Take all you want. But you'd better come back in the spring when the work is done."

"That's a great idea," Nate said. "Do an 'after' article. I'll bet you could sell it to some regional magazines with pictures of the lodge the way it is now and with the updates. That would bring Jeff a lot of business."

"You may be right." Emily began a mental list of publications to query about the story as they strolled to the back of the first floor.

"My quarters are back here, behind the office," Jeff said. "But this room is open to the guests. It's our library." He ushered them into a side room, and Emily knew at once it was her favorite part of the lodge. Immediately she wanted to curl up with a book in one of the overstuffed chairs before the fieldstone fireplace. The old wainscoting of wide cherry boards gave the room a warm, cozy feeling.

"What a beautiful spot!"

Jeff smiled. "This was the original owner's sitting room, but it was too nice to keep for my personal use. It's the one room in this place that's not stark. Old Eberhardt wanted a comfortable place in the middle of the long Maine winters, I guess."

"Who's Eberhardt?" Emily took out her little notebook.

"He was the lumberman who built this place. The old boss." Jeff stooped to touch a match to the kindling laid in the fireplace.

"Do you know much about him?"

"Some. There's a legend about him. His death, actually. I'll tell you in the morning when you're getting the pictures."

Emily put on an exaggerated scowl. "You're going to make me wait until morning to hear the story?"

Nate laughed. "She's always been that way. Impatient."

Jeff sat down and gestured for them to do the same. "Make yourselves comfortable. Well, I could tell you now, but if you want to sleep tonight, you'd better wait."

"Oooh. It's a ghost story." Emily knew

then that the tale was probably half history, half nonsense, but she also knew the selling power of a good New England legend.

Jeff turned to Nate with a smile still playing on his lips. "We'll get to that tomorrow. You said you're going into police work, Nate. That will be quite a change from running the marina."

"I think I'm going to like it." Nate's smile lit up his face, and Emily felt a surge of pride for him. "I started at the academy a couple of weeks ago."

Jeff shook his head. "It's not for me. I'd rather run the lodge than chase criminals. Does this decision have anything to do with the murder you and Emily helped solve last summer?"

"Sort of. I've wanted to be a cop since junior high, but I had to put things on hold when my dad got sick. Last summer reminded me of how much I'd wanted this."

The talk soon turned to the village of Baxter and its residents, their families, and Emily's former work as a journalist in Connecticut. After an hour, they turned in for the night.

Emily settled beneath the cozy quilt on her bed and sighed as her head met the pillow. At least Jeff had invested in modern mattresses for the guest rooms. She was sure she wouldn't hear a thing for at least eight hours.

Nate jerked awake. It was dark, and his heart pounded. What noise had startled him out of sleep? The pale rectangle that was his window gave him enough light to fumble on the nightstand for his watch. He pressed the button to illuminate the dial. One thirty. A thump and then a tapping sound came from . . . where? Below him? Jeff must be up.

Nate lay back on the pillow but knew he couldn't go back to sleep. He, Emily, and Jeff were supposed to be the only three in the lodge tonight. Jeff had said he was tired. What had gotten him up again?

He stood up and waved his arm in the darkness until his hand struck the teardrop prism on the end of the light string, and he pulled it. Light flooded the room.

More thuds from downstairs, followed by a shout.

Nate yanked on his jeans and tore down the hall to the stairway.

Jeff stood at the bottom of the stairs in the lobby area, a pistol in his hand.

"What happened?" Nate whispered, stealing down the stairs.

Light spilled from an open door down the hallway beyond the office, and he could make out his friend's pale face in the semidarkness. Jeff's curly, almost black hair was rumpled, and his eyes flashed as he sent a probing gaze over the quiet lobby.

"I heard someone thumping around." Nate reached the bottom step. "I heard it, too. Maybe one of your staff came in?"

"Nobody's due tonight. They'd have called me if they were coming in."

"It sounded like somebody tripped and fell," Nate said.

Jeff turned and looked over the dining area. "Someone's prowling around in here."

Excitement prickled down Nate's neck. He didn't wish for danger, but he couldn't help the rush of adrenaline that intrigue brought. "The sound came from beneath my room."

Jeff nodded. "Let's search the first floor. Grab a flashlight from the stand by the front door."

Nate tiptoed to the entry, pulled a flashlight from the drawer Jeff had indicated, and rejoined him by the stairs. He eyed the pistol warily.

"Is that thing loaded?"

"Yeah, but don't worry. I'll be careful. I think the noise came from this direction." Jeff gestured toward the kitchen and took the lead, his gun raised.

They crept down the dim hallway toward the back of the building. Jeff held Nate back and stepped to one side of the kitchen doorway. He reached around the jamb to flip a switch, and light flooded the kitchen.

Silence greeted them, and Jeff stepped in cautiously, leading with the pistol. Nate followed, and they quickly looked under tables and behind fixtures. Jeff checked the lock on the back door.

"Nothing here," Nate whispered.

"There's gotta be —"

A soft sound came from somewhere beyond the room, and Jeff stiffened.

"A window?" Nate asked. The sound reminded him of the noise his bedroom window in the old house by the marina made when he slid the casing up.

Jeff ran past him to the hall and through another door. Nate strode after him into the library. Frigid air blasted through the open window. Jeff hurried to it and leaned out.

Nate heard crashing and twigs snapping in the underbrush on the edge of the woods. "See anything?" he asked as he crossed the room.

"He's gone." Jeff drew back from the window, shaking his head in disgust. "But I saw someone, all right. From the back. I'm pretty sure it was a man." He closed the window and switched on the overhead light.

Something small and metallic against the base of the window seat caught Nate's eye. He knelt on the floor to get a better look, but he didn't pick it up.

"What you got there?" Jeff asked.

"Pocketknife," said Nate.

Jeff got down beside him.

The knife was about three inches long with a dark, purplish-red case.

"It's not yours?"

"No," said Jeff. "I have four or five of them that belonged to my father in my desk. But none of them looks like that."

"Good. At least we have some kind of evidence. Have you had intruders before?"

"Never."

Nate got to his feet again. He wondered what kind of valuables Jeff kept in the lodge and if they were locked up.

"Probably some tramp looking for food," Jeff said. "Still, I'd better check the safe."

A safe? Nate began to imagine what might be kept there. He thought even a rumor of a safe in the old lodge might tempt potential thieves. He thought of Baxter resident Rocky Vigue's escapades with stolen electronics the summer before.

Suddenly there was a creaking noise from upstairs, and Jeff stiffened.

"Emily," said Nate. "She must have heard something, too, and woken up. I'd better tell her what's going on."

"Good idea," said Jeff. He took one more look around the room before heading to his office.

Nate found Emily coming down the stairs in blue jeans and a red wool sweater, her feet bare, brandishing a heavy silver flashlight. He couldn't help smiling at the picture she made — a little like Miss Scarlet from the game of Clue, the large flashlight in place of the lead pipe or the candlestick.

"What's going on? I heard noises," she whispered. "And what are you laughing at?" She reached the bottom of the stairs and stood close to him.

"Miss Scarlet on the staircase with the flashlight." He tried to stifle his laughter.

She narrowed her eyes playfully. "Very funny. This flashlight happens to be my weapon of choice."

"It's about as big as you are."

"Yes, and it doesn't work, either. I found it in the closet in my room." She frowned as she shook it. Then she looked up at him. "So, was that you I heard bumping around?"

"Someone broke in."

Her eyes flickered. "What happened? Was it a burglary?"

Nate squeezed her hand. "We're not sure yet. Everything seems to be fine, but Jeff's calling the police."

"Wow. I'm glad he didn't tell us that ghost story last night after all. Waking up to strange noises was bad enough without a poltergeist on my mind."

"Yeah," said Nate. "I don't believe in ghosts, but this rambling old lodge can be pretty creepy at night, I'll admit."

"Did you see the intruder? What did he look like?" Emily had shifted into reporter mode, which meant she wasn't frightened. That was a relief.

"By the time we realized what was happening, he was climbing out the library window. Jeff saw him running into the woods."

"Was anything taken?"

"Not sure. Jeff mentioned a safe. I assume it's in his office."

Emily nodded. "I definitely heard some thumping, or stomping around." She stifled a yawn. "What time is it?"

"About two. Not much point in going back to bed if the police are coming."

They moved into the living room area, where Emily found the pull for the light fixture and tugged it. "It doesn't look as though they touched anything in here." She sat down on a leather-covered sofa.

Nate watched her as she ran a hand through her disheveled hair. She looked pretty, even though her eyelids were still heavy from sleep. "Em, I'm sorry our weekend's started off so crazy. I was hoping for a peaceful getaway." He eased himself onto the sofa beside her, putting an arm around her shoulders.

Emily laughed softly. "There's nothing you could have done to prevent someone from breaking in here during the night. Anyway, I don't mind. You know I like adventures. And I'm not worried about anything with you here."

He smiled. That was something he loved

26

about Emily. She wasn't a sissy, but she also seemed to be getting used to the idea of letting him take care of her.

Jeff walked in. "The police are on their way. I had a look at the safe, and it's intact. Nothing seems to have been touched."

"We didn't notice anything out of place either," said Emily.

Jeff looked around and nodded. "Sorry to wake you up."

"No problem. I wouldn't want to miss out on the excitement."

Nate flashed Jeff a smile. *That's my girl,* he thought.

"It could be an hour before they get here," said Jeff. "Do you two want coffee?"

"Sounds good," said Nate.

Emily nodded. "I second that, if it's decaf."

A few minutes later, with steaming cups of coffee in hand and a box of cheese crackers Jeff had dug out of the cupboard over the range top, they all sat down in the lobby to wait for the police to arrive.

"So, tell us more about the crazy old guy who built this place," Nate said.

Emily punched his shoulder. "He wasn't crazy. He was probably very smart. He was a lumber baron."

"Well, he didn't have electricity. That's crazy."

Jeff laughed. "His name was Alexander Eberhardt, and he was a bit eccentric, from what I've heard, but not crazy. I'm thinking about having his story written up for an ad. I might post it on the Web site for the lodge. Something people can read online. Think that would draw in customers?"

"If it's creepy enough. You said something about his death," Emily prompted.

"Mmm. His mysterious death and the missing Eberhardt treasure."

"Wait, let me get my notebook!" Emily jumped up, but before she reached the bottom of the stairs, lights flashed over the walls of the lobby and tires crunched on the gravel outside.

Jeff welcomed the sheriff's deputy at the front door.

"Hey, you made good time."

"Yeah, I was in Aswontee when dispatch called me. Evening, folks." He nodded at Nate and Emily.

Nate recognized him as Russell Young, one of the men he would work with when his stint at the police academy was over. He stepped forward and shook Young's hand. Jeff guided the deputy toward the library, and Nate hesitated.

"Oh, come on," Emily whispered. "I want to hear what they say, too."

Nate grinned and tiptoed after the men. He and Emily stopped in the doorway just in time to see Young pick up the pocketknife and put it in an evidence bag.

"Will you check it for fingerprints?" Jeff asked.

"Well, I tell you," Young said, "it's pretty small, and you don't think anything was stolen. Truth is, we probably won't bother."

Emily's lips skewed in a scowl, and Nate slipped his arm around her.

Young smiled at Jeff. "Now, if you had a dead body lying here, that would be different, right, Nate?"

"Oh yeah," Nate said. "We'd send that knife for prints, and we might even give the state police a call."

Young barked a laugh, and even Emily cracked a smile. They all knew that the sheriff's department was not allowed to handle homicides. The Maine State Police took those over except in the state's two largest cities, Portland and Bangor. Baxter, Maine, was far too small to have its own police department, let alone a homicide squad.

"I will ask around," Young said. "We have a few known thieves in the area. I'll see if all of them have alibis for tonight, though it's usually pretty hard to prove a guy wasn't in his own bed at 2:00 a.m."

Jeff's disappointment showed in his hangdog expression. He offered the deputy coffee, but Young turned it down and wished them all a good night as he headed for the door.

"Sorry I couldn't do more, folks, but you scared him off. At least no one was hurt. That's what's important."

"Thanks, Russ," Nate called after him. He turned to face Jeff. "He's right, you know. That burglar will probably never come back."

"Ready to go back to sleep?" Nate asked. They stood at the front window of the comfortable lobby, watching the police car's taillights disappear down the long driveway.

"I'm so wound up now, I doubt I'll get back to sleep." Emily turned to look at their host. "Why don't you tell us the rest of the story about Alexander Eberhardt, Jeff?"

"All right, but let me get a refill on my coffee. You want more?"

"Not me," said Emily. "But if you have any hot chocolate mix . . ."

"Come on. I'm sure we do."

They fixed their hot drinks in the kitchen

and then moved into the snug library, where the burglar had made his getaway. Jeff raked up the embers of last evening's fire and added several sticks of wood.

"Might as well make good use of the fireplace."

"It is a little chilly in here." Emily curled her feet up on the sofa and leaned toward Nate until her shoulder touched his.

"It costs me a mint to heat this place in winter," Jeff said. "I'm hoping to have a better insulating job done when the wiring is completed."

When the fire blazed, he dropped into an overstuffed armchair.

"Well, like I told you, Mr. Eberhardt built this lodge as the barracks for his lumbering crew. I think he had other lumber camps, too, and he made a huge success of it. He was getting along in years, and in 1901, he sold his company. It was in the middle of the logging season. He went from here to Bangor by sleigh in January to close the sale. Supposedly he picked up the payment for the business and the payroll for the last disbursement to his employees before handing the company over to the new owner. There were about forty lumberjacks staying here at the lodge then, working through the winter. A lot of them were French Canadians, and from what my father told me, there would also have been a clerk, several teamsters, and a cook."

"Quite an operation," Nate said.

"Yeah. The story goes that Mr. Eberhardt paid his crews once a month. In winter, the 'boys' would get one day off after payday. They could go into Baxter or Aswontee if they wanted and spend some of their pay. A few would have Mr. Eberhardt send the bulk of their wages home for them the next time he went to Bangor."

"That must have been a rough life." Emily sipped her cocoa and nestled closer to Nate.

Nate stretched his arm across the back of the couch behind her. "It'd be almost as bad as going to sea, I'd think. Away from their families all winter."

"Yeah, they would stay in the lumber camps for six or eight months," Jeff agreed. "They say there was a big storm the day after Mr. Eberhardt left. He had a man with him to drive the sleigh. When the snow started, all the lumberjacks were disappointed because they figured he would be delayed. If he stayed overnight in Bangor, they wouldn't get their pay on the usual day. But . . ."

Emily watched him, enthralled by the

story. She could easily imagine the big men snowed in by the blizzard, fretting and pacing because the boss was late returning.

Jeff raised his eyebrows and leaned forward. "The next morning, Mr. Eberhardt was found in his bed in the lodge — in the room I sleep in now."

"So he made it through in the sleigh." Nate nodded in satisfaction, and Jeff sat back and let his shoulders droop.

"Well, yeah. Unfortunately, he was dead."

Emily let out a little gasp, trying to work out the puzzle of how the man had died and yet made it safely into his own bed.

"There was no doctor," Jeff said. "André, the man who drove him to Bangor and back, assured the other men that the boss was alive, though fatigued and chilled, when they got in late the previous night. André was as shocked as they were — or so he claimed — when he heard Mr. Eberhardt was dead. The crew didn't know what to think of it, but they probably surmised he had suffered a heart attack after his strenuous trek through the storm."

"It works for me," Nate said.

"Oh, come on." Emily swiveled her head to look at him in disbelief. "That's too convenient."

Jeff grinned. "There's more."

"I knew it." Emily settled back to listen.

"The snow continued, and the men decided they'd better build a coffin and put Mr. Eberhardt's body in it. They decided to put him out in the woodshed until they could get to town and send a message to his kin. That way the body wouldn't — well, you know."

Emily grimaced, and Jeff went on.

"The clerk wasn't sure what to do, but he decided to go ahead and pay the men. But when he opened the safe —"

"The money was gone!" Emily laughed but sobered quickly as Jeff shook his head.

"The payroll was there, enough for each man's wages. But the payment for the business and all Mr. Eberhardt's timber acreage, amounting to about 140,000 dollars in cash, was missing."

"Why would he bring that much cash with him to the lumber camp?" Emily asked. "Wouldn't he have put it in the bank in Bangor?"

"He was supposedly going to retire and head for his old home in Houlton when the new owner came, so he took his money with him. In fact, André told them the boss had the money with him when they arrived the night before. He claimed he saw the boss open the safe before he left him for the night."

"Well, duh," said Emily. "Of course he opened the safe. The payroll was in there."

"What did the lumberjacks do?" Nate asked.

"The men searched the lodge, the sleigh, and the barn."

"I should hope they raked that André guy over the coals," Emily said.

"Oh yes, André was questioned so much, he got angry. The other men seemed to suspect him, not only of making off with the money, but of doing something to Mr. Eberhardt as well."

"I should think so!" She waited, knowing the story wasn't over.

Jeff dropped his voice to a spooky whisper. "The money was never found, and when the blizzard was over, André disappeared."

"They just let him walk away?" Nate asked. That didn't sit right with Emily, either.

Jeff shrugged. "I don't know what happened to him. I don't think anyone does. But in my family the suspicion is that André took the money and got away with it. And murder."

They sat in silence for a moment. Emily watched the snapping logs in the fire. "I wish I'd been here then."

"No, you don't," said Nate.

"You'd have been scared," Jeff agreed with a smile.

She shook her head then scowled. "Okay, maybe I would be scared, but I'd still try to find out what happened. I wonder . . ."

"What?" Jeff asked.

She threw him an apologetic smile. "I wonder a lot of things. Could Mr. Eberhardt have hidden the money someplace besides the safe that night? And did they just let André leave? Or did he sneak out without them seeing him? A hundred forty thousand dollars is a lot of money. I can't imagine the other men letting him leave with a bulging knapsack."

"Maybe he hid it somewhere outside the lodge and picked it up when he left." Nate waited expectantly for her to comment on his theory.

She nodded. "Possible. Or maybe someone else did it and framed André. When he left, the others quit looking for a thief because they assumed André was it."

Nate leaned forward and seized her hand. "Hey, what if André did do it and another man caught him with the money, did André in, and stashed the loot for himself?"

Jeff shrugged and let out a deep chuckle.

"You guys are too much. The most likely scenario is that Mr. Eberhardt died of natural causes. The theft of the money could have been a crime of opportunity. The boss keeled over, and André — or someone else, as you say — saw the chance to get his hands on a fortune."

"That would have been a huge fortune in those days," Nate said.

"I'll say. People would kill for less than that nowadays." Emily yawned. "I suppose we should try to sleep for a few hours. But I know I'll be thinking about old André and the money now."

Jeff laughed. "Yeah, I'd better hit the sack. My staff is due to start arriving around 8:00 a.m., and our first guests will come in around one. We'll be scrambling to be ready for business."

"What else do you need to do?" Nate asked. "Everything's clean."

"For one thing, we'll be getting in fresh food supplies, and the cook will start getting supper ready. Just preparing the evening meal will keep three people busy most of the day. And the guides will go over their equipment. The maids will open up the guest rooms and make sure they're warm and welcoming."

Nate stood and held out a hand to Emily.

"Sounds like you work as hard as the lumberjacks used to."

"Almost." Jeff stirred the coals in the fireplace and went to check the lock on the window casement. Emily gathered their mugs.

"I wonder a lot of things about tonight, too," she said as they walked to the kitchen. "I wonder what that guy was after, and how he got in, and why he dropped his knife, and —"

"And if he'll try again." Jeff's grim expression chilled her.

3

Nate awoke to smells of strong coffee and frying bacon. His watch told him he'd slept until half past eight, but he still felt sleepy. He hurried into his clothes and took his shaving gear to the bathroom down the hall. When he emerged a few minutes later, Emily was just leaving her room.

"Hey! Smells like breakfast." She waited for him, and Nate joined her at the top of the stairs.

"Sleep all right?" He stooped to kiss her cheek.

"Yes. I didn't think I would, but I dropped off almost as soon as I got back to bed."

They found Jeff in the dining room, seated at a table set for three. With a cup of coffee at his elbow, he skimmed a newspaper, and Nate noticed that his host had both the *Baxter Journal* and the *Bangor Daily News.*

"Plenty of reading material, I see."

Jeff jumped up with a smile. "Yeah, I was

just reading Emily's story about the play they're putting on at the high school next weekend."

Her face lit up. "It's really good. I was at the rehearsal the other night, and the kids are doing a great job. *Peter Pan.* The boy who plays Hook has a fantastic voice."

"I'll have to tell the guests," Jeff said. "Some of them might want to drive to Aswontee to see it Saturday night."

The kitchen door opened, and a middle-aged woman wearing a huge white apron came in with a platter in each hand.

"Good morning, folks!"

Jeff said, "Nate, Emily, this is my cook, Lucille. She got in about an hour ago and offered to take over for me in the kitchen. I think it hurt her to see me trying to cook bacon."

"Now, now, you were doing a good job. I just thought you'd like to relax with your guests." Lucille smiled at them.

"It certainly looks and smells delicious," Emily said.

"Can I get you folks some orange juice?" Lucille asked. "Or are you like the boss and go straight for the coffee?"

"Juice for me, please," Emily said, and Nate accepted some, too.

When Lucille had left them again, Jeff

asked the blessing. They helped themselves to the eggs, bacon, and blueberry muffins.

Nate took a big bite of his muffin and closed his eyes. "Emily, don't tell Mom, but these are as good as hers."

"Oh boy." She glanced at Jeff. "That's a big compliment to your cook."

Nate seldom bothered to fix himself a big breakfast. Once in a while he ventured over to the parsonage and ate with his mother and Pastor Jared Phillips, his stepfather, but he missed his mother's cooking and just knowing she would be in the kitchen every morning.

"You've got a gem in Lucille," he said.

Jeff grinned. "I know. I pay her as much as I can afford. I'm constantly worried she'll go to some fancy restaurant in Bangor. But she's been with me three years now. She and her husband live in Aswontee. If the weather gets bad in winter, she stays over here. And I insisted she bring George out for a week on the house last summer to enjoy the lake and the fishing."

"If you keep her happy, she'll stay," Emily said.

"That's the idea. Without a good cook, a sporting camp may as well fold up."

A young woman came in from the lobby and approached their table. She nodded at

Nate and Emily but focused her attention on her boss.

"Excuse me, Jeff, the Beverly party would like to check in early."

"Are they here?"

"No, they're in Bangor. Mr. Beverly called on his cell phone. They can be here in an hour, and they're raring to go."

Jeff rose and tossed his napkin on the table. "All right. Tell them to come ahead. I'll have to speak with Mac. He's guiding their hunt tomorrow. They'll want to go over their route with him. And Lucille will have to plan on a guest lunch. That will thrill her. Excuse me, Nate and Emily. I wanted to hike with you this morning, but it looks like I'll be busy. Make yourselves at home, and feel free to use any of our equipment."

"I was hoping to ask Jeff some more questions about Alexander Eberhardt," Emily said when he had left the room.

"I think he told us everything he knows last night."

She nodded. "I'd like to write up the story for him. But I'd need to do some research first."

"You think you can document a legend?" Nate eyed her keenly. Emily had a wonderful mind, the kind that sorted and probed and wrestled with details until she inevitably came up with a complicated, intriguing story and expressed it in such simple words that any child could understand it, yet so beautifully that it touched people's hearts. It was a gift; he recognized that.

Her face tensed as she pondered his question, and he knew her brain cells were clicking.

"I think I'll run to Bangor next week and see if I can dig up anything at the newspaper morgue. There's got to be something about the lumber company and Eberhardt. And I should at least be able to find an obituary, if not a story, about his mysterious death."

"Go for it," Nate said. "Personally, I'd rather think about the little mystery we got into last night."

"That was scary," she admitted. "I'm glad you and Jeff were both here."

They went up to their rooms for their outdoor clothing and spent the morning hiking through the woods behind the lodge. The trail they chose rose steeply to the summit of a rocky hill. When they reached a high ledge, a vista of Blue Heron Lake opened to them, and they stood for a long time looking out over the choppy, gray water.

"I'm glad I'm not out in a boat today,"

Nate said.

Emily shivered, although her down parka kept her warm. "Think it'll snow?"

"Could."

"Well, I'm glad I'm not going out bear hunting. Lakeview Lodge is a pretty cozy place."

"Does that mean you're ready to turn back?" Nate asked.

"Not yet, but keep this in mind: If we get a blinding blizzard, I'd rather sit by the fireplace than put on the snowshoes."

Lunch surpassed Nate's expectations, and he forayed into the kitchen to give Lucille his compliments on the homemade soup, fruit salad, and rolls. He and Emily poked around the old lodge once more, staying out of the traffic as new guests arrived. Emily carried her camera and notebook and jotted down her impressions of the rustic architecture and the views from the porch and various windows. Meanwhile, Nate mentally catalogued all the repairs Jeff had in store. Yes, it was time for some modernization. Past time. Emily snapped photos on her digital camera, documenting the details and the overall atmosphere.

"Oh, Nate, just look at the handmade chairs on the side porch." She raised her camera. "I'm going to ask Jeff's permission to query some of the regional magazines. If I sold an article to *Down East* or *Yankee,* he'd get a lot of attention."

"You think they'd buy a story about a place like this?"

"Sure. A family business with an antique building and a legend. A legend is as good as a ghost for human interest."

Nate still felt a little skeptical, but Emily had more experience in hooking editors than he did. He opened a door off the lobby.

"Jeff told me this room is kept for handicapped people. It's the only guest room on the ground floor."

"He's not going to put in an elevator, is he?" Emily asked with a frown. "That would be awfully expensive."

"No, but he wants to have the ramp on the side of the building extended. And he's talking about someday installing a swimming pool."

"What do they need with a pool? They have the lake."

Nate shrugged. "Some people don't like to swim in the weeds and muck, I guess. No leeches in a pool. No minnows to nibble your toes."

"I love swimming in the lake." Emily's jaw jutted out, and he couldn't help smiling.

"Of course you do. You grew up in Baxter.

But you've got to admit, the water stays freezing cold until well into June, and the swimming season is awfully short. If Jeff had a heated pool, people could swim a lot longer."

"He wouldn't build an indoor pool, would he?"

"I doubt it. That would be an astronomical expense. Anyway, he says the pool will have to wait two or three years, until he recovers from the cost of remodeling."

"He could get a hot tub." Emily clicked a photo of the deep-silled window in the guest room. "These walls have got to be a foot and a half thick."

Nate nodded. "Jeff says there are a lot of crawl spaces and cubby holes, which will make things easier for the electricians and insulators."

When they went back to the lobby, Lisa, the young woman manning the desk and phone, called to them.

"Mr. Holman, Jeff wondered if you two would like to join one of the guides who's going to take some supplies to a cabin he has a few miles away. One of our hunting parties will be staying there for the next two nights, and Jeff wants the beds set up and the food supplies in place before they get there."

Nate and Emily accepted and were soon bumping over a woods road in a Jeep with Robert "Mac" MacBriarty, one of Jeff's top guides. All the way to the cabin, Emily peppered Mac with questions about his job, the process of earning a guide's license, and the eccentric guests he served. She and Nate helped him set up the cabin, where the hunters would stay without benefit of electricity or running water.

"I don't know," Emily said as she looked around the small building. "Camping in winter."

"They've got a woodstove," Nate reminded her. "Besides, it's not officially winter for another month."

"It's still cold." She shivered.

MacBriarty laughed. "Mostly we get men on hunts, especially this time of year. Not many women roughing it on a deer hunt."

A light snow began to fall as they drove back to the lodge, and Emily cuddled into the curve of Nate's arm. *Perfect,* he thought.

After supper, Nate suggested they again take a walk. The sky had cleared, and the moon shone dazzlingly over the lake.

"I was sort of hoping we could do the hot-chocolate-and-fireplace thing again," Emily admitted.

"Oh, come on. You're an active girl. Just a

short walk, and Lucille will give us hot cocoa afterward."

"And marshmallows?"

He laughed and reached for her hand, pulling her up out of her chair. "I promise."

The snow had stopped, leaving an inch of pure white on every surface. Nate scooped up a handful and tried to form a snowball, but the snow was too dry.

"Powder." He brushed his gloved hands together.

"The ski resort owners will be glad," Emily said.

They walked out onto the wooden wharf, where the fishermen docked in summer, and gazed across the lake. The water was smooth now. In the far distance, Nate could see the dark bulk of Grand Cat Island, where Emily's summer cottage was, and off to the right twinkled a few lights in the town of Baxter, on the lake's eastern shore.

"It's beautiful here," Emily sighed. "I'm so glad I came back to Maine."

"Me, too." Nate put his arm around her, but the moment was less romantic than he'd hoped, with both their bulky coats and thick gloves between them. "I got you something, Em."

She looked up into his face. "You did?"

"Mmm-hmmm." When he stooped to kiss

her, Emily's lips were frosty cold. He kept it short and hugged her. "I guess that hot cocoa wouldn't be so bad right about now. Unless a lot of other people are in the library, that is."

"Don't change the subject. What did you get me?"

He chuckled and pulled off one glove and reached into his jacket pocket. What if he dropped it into the lake? He glanced back along the dock to the shore. That wasn't much better. He could lose it in the snow.

"Let's go in." He took her hand and pulled her toward the lodge.

When they hit the snow-covered turf at the end of the dock, Emily dug her heels in.

"Wait a second, buster. You're the one who wanted to come out here. You can't just —"

Nate laughed. "I promise you won't regret it."

She walked along beside him then. "Is it a present?"

"Sort of."

"What do you mean, sort of?"

"You'll see."

They entered by the side door and stamped the snow off their low boots. Nate took her coat and hung it on a rack of hooks near the door. Hand in hand they crossed the lobby and went around the corner to the library door.

Emily stopped on the threshold and turned around.

"People," she whispered. "Do you still want to go in?"

Nate frowned. There had to be someplace private. "Wait here a minute."

He found Jeff in the kitchen going over the next day's menus with Lucille and her helper, Carrie. Jeff and the kitchen staff were more than willing to enter into his scheme.

Five minutes later, Nate went back to the library. Emily was seated on an ottoman, chatting with a group of four hunters, all older men. She seemed to be letting them tell her their favorite hunting stories, and Nate was sure they appreciated having a new audience for their tales. He waited in the doorway while one of them concluded his anecdote. Warmth spread through him as he watched her. It had taken these fellows only minutes to fall in love with her, and he knew that exact feeling. Emily . . . the perfect listener, the sweetest companion, the dearest friend he'd ever known.

She looked up and smiled at him as he entered.

"Sorry, gents," he said to the others. "I'm going to steal her away from you."

"Aw, no fair," one white-haired man protested.

"Come back again, Emily," said another.

"Where are we going?" she asked as Nate led her back toward the lobby.

Nate smiled. "A special spot on loan from the owner."

He took her past the front desk and paused at a doorway.

"Oh. Isn't this Jeff's private suite?"

Nate grinned. "Exactly — the key word being *private*. Jeff says we can use his sitting room." He swung the door open, and Emily entered, still holding his hand.

She caught her breath. "Wow. This is as good as the library."

"Better. No hunters in here. But Jeff told me he had it redecorated last summer."

Emily nodded, her blue eyes sparkling. This was the one part of the lodge Jeff hadn't included in his tour. His private living room was small but comfortable, with a sofa, armchair, and entertainment center. Colorful cushions and rugs, accented by hunting prints and a patchwork hanging on the walls, brightened the room, but the focal point was a fieldstone fireplace, smaller than the one in the library.

In the few minutes Nate had given them, Jeff had lit the fire and Lucille had delivered

51

a pot of cocoa with two mugs and spoons and a dish of marshmallows on the side.

"I love it!" Emily slid onto the sofa and reached for the teapot. She pulled her hand back and sobered as Nate sat down beside her and slipped his arm around her. "I love you," she whispered.

Perfect, he thought again. He leaned over and kissed her lightly. "You want your present now, sweetheart?"

"You mean this isn't it?"

"No, this is just the window dressing." His voice caught, and her eyes flickered, as though she sensed the moment was more serious than she'd foreseen.

"In that case, I'd love to see it."

Nate sat very still as he realized where he'd left the box.

"What?" she asked after a moment.

He managed a smile. "Hold on a sec. I . . . left it in my jacket pocket."

He dashed through the lobby to the coatrack and retrieved it then tried to walk back to Jeff's quarters calmly. Jeff was leaning against the front desk talking to Lisa, and they both grinned at him.

Emily had poured mugs full of hot chocolate and piled several marshmallows into hers.

He sat down and took a deep breath.

"So," she said.

"Yeah." Suddenly everything he'd planned to say drifted up the chimney with the wood smoke. "Uh . . ." He fingered the little square box. "Em, I . . ."

All sorts of thoughts came to him, none of them helpful at first. At last he focused in on her face, expectant and patient. Emily, the perfect listener . . . Emily, the dearest friend . . .

"I love you." It was a start.

Her smile burst out, and anticipation washed through him. It was a good start.

"Emily . . ." Taking courage, he reached for her hands, fumbled with the little box, and set it on the table. "I've loved you for ages. You know that. Half my life, at least. I don't want to go on without you. I know we'll have to make a lot of . . . Aw, Em, will you marry me?"

As he got the last line out, he slid to his knees beside the sofa and looked deep into her soft blue eyes.

Her lower lip quivered. She reached up and ran her fingers through his hair. "Yes. Of course I will! You know I love you to distraction." She bent toward him, and he kissed her. Hope and satisfaction and joy exploded inside him. He found the kneeling posture suddenly awkward and rose to sit with her again, pulling her into his arms.

"Is it as good as that old dream you used to have about us?"

She closed her eyes, but a smile hovered on her lips. "Better. I think this is as good as it gets in this life."

Nate sighed and held her close. "No, you're wrong there. It's going to get better and better."

"It couldn't possibly."

"Not even if you open the box?"

She sat up. "I almost forgot. Is it . . . ?"

Nate winked at her and put on a Humphrey Bogart voice. "It ain't marshmallows, shweetheart."

She laughed, and he reached for the box. All week, since he'd bought it at the jewelry store in Waterville, near the academy, he'd agonized over whether he'd made the right choice.

"If you don't like it . . ."

"Show me."

He gulped and sprang the catch. She stared down at the sparkling ring.

"I love it."

She took the ring carefully from its velvet-lined box, and Nate helped her slide it onto her finger.

"It's wonderful," she breathed.

She dove into his arms, and Nate kissed

her again, reveling in the moment.
  Perfect!

4

Emily spread the latest edition of the *Baxter Journal* out on her desk in the newspaper's stark office. "This looks fabulous, Felicia. I love the way you arranged the photos." She held up the paper, showcasing her sparkling diamond against the newsprint, wondering how long it would take her friend, coworker, and temporary roommate to notice the ring.

Felicia looked up from her desk, smiling from behind the large coffee mug she held poised at her mouth. She never wore makeup, and her hazel eyes seemed to get lost behind her thick glasses. "Thanks. The phone's been ringing off the hook all morning." She still seemed oblivious to the real reason for Emily's excitement. "Everyone wants to know more about the lost treasure."

"I do, too," said Emily. "Has it been a bother, though?"

"Not really. I refer them to Jeff."

Emily laughed. "Then I feel bad for him. I hope it's not keeping him from his renovations."

"Well, I have to admit, you were right about the human interest in that story. Let's hope the other business profiles go as well."

The phone rang.

"And there's another one." Felicia set down her coffee. "*Baxter Journal,* Felicia Chadwick speaking. Yes, she's here. Hold on."

Emily stepped over to Felicia's desk and deliberately took the phone with her left hand.

"It's Jeff," Felicia whispered.

Emily nodded. "Hi, Jeff."

"Hey there, Emily. Just wanted to thank you for your spread in the *Journal.* Your article is amazing."

"Thanks. I hope I did the lodge justice."

"You certainly did. I really like the picture you took of the north side. You must have been standing in the woods to get that angle."

"I've learned to get creative," said Emily.

"Your story's great for business. I've had several calls from people asking about the legend."

"I hope it hasn't been a bother for you." Emily switched the receiver to her right hand, leaned against the edge of Felicia's desk, and rested her left hand beside the computer keyboard. She drummed her fingers on the desk.

"Are you kidding? I'm now booked solid for the month after reopening!"

"That's super, Jeff. I'm glad I could help you out with publicity."

"You sure have. Speaking of publicity, would you mind if I put your article on the Web site I made for the lodge?"

"Go right ahead."

"Thanks a million, Emily."

"So," Felicia said when Emily had hung up, leaning back in her chair and staring at Emily expectantly through her glasses, "what about that ring?"

"You did notice!"

"Girl, I noticed. I've been in the newspaper game long enough. I see all."

Emily beamed.

"And if you ask me, it's about time that man proposed. Let's hear the story."

Emily wheeled over the chair from her desk and sat across from Felicia. "It all began on a snowy day at a haunted lumberjack lodge . . ."

Felicia raised her eyebrows in mock surprise. "I knew there had to be more to this lodge story."

■ ■ ■ ■

That evening Emily had just settled down on the sofa in Felicia's living room with a bowl of Cheerios and a stack of *Yankee* magazines when the phone rang. "I'll get it!" She jumped up.

Felicia laughed. "Be my guest."

Emily grabbed the phone. "Hello?"

"Hi, Emily, it's Mom. How's the bride-to-be?"

"I'm great, Mom. Nate's coming up from the academy this weekend, and he should be here in a few hours."

"Good, because I wanted to ask you about Christmas," said her mother. "I was hoping you two would come down to Brunswick."

"I'd love to, Mom! And I'm sure Nate will agree. He may want to spend Christmas Eve here with his mom and Pastor Phillips, but we should be able to come down the next morning. It wouldn't be Christmas without your gingersnaps and those cute little celery wagons."

"Okay, honey, you tell Nate I'm cooking a huge dinner with celery wagons, and I expect you both in Brunswick on Christmas day."

Emily smiled. "I'll do that."

59

"How's it working out with Felcia?"

"It's going fine. She has a small house, but I've pretty much got the upstairs to myself, so I have plenty of room. I'm glad she offered to let me stay here until I can move back to the cottage for the summer."

They chatted for another ten minutes as Emily told her more about rooming with Felicia for the winter, the story she'd written on the lodge, and some of her ideas for the wedding.

When Nate arrived in Baxter, Emily was brimming with anticipation. She skipped down the steps as he parked his SUV in the driveway, and waited eagerly for him to emerge.

"Wow, look at you," he said, climbing out of the vehicle. "What are you so excited about?"

"I'm excited because I haven't seen you all week." Emily threw her arms around him. "And I missed you!"

"I missed you, too, Em." He squeezed her, and she pulled away, tugging him toward the steps.

"Come on in. I want to show you what I did this afternoon."

Nate went into the little house with her and greeted Felicia. Emily impatiently waited for him to join her in the living area.

When he sat down beside her on the sofa, she put a sheaf of papers in his hands.

"What's this?" he asked.

"Printouts from the courthouse. Remember how that sheriff's deputy said there are a few known thieves living in this area?"

"Yeah."

"Well, I asked the clerk at the courthouse to print out a list for me of all the crimes committed in the town of Baxter or by a Baxter resident in the past two years."

Nate eyed the papers dubiously. "What good will that do?"

"It will tell us who the known criminals are, and we can check up on them."

Nate looked almost as though his stomach hurt. "Aw, Em, don't you think we should let the sheriff's department handle this?"

"You heard the deputy. He practically said they won't do anything."

"No, sweetheart, that's not what he said."

"Well, he said they wouldn't dust for fingerprints."

"Because nothing was stolen from the lodge."

Emily huffed out a breath in frustration. "But there would have been if you and Jeff hadn't scared the burglar off. So I thought that we could look over this list and see who in Baxter has been known to break into

61

houses before, and —"

Nate tapped the papers with a finger. "I see you've already highlighted the major suspects."

"Well, yeah." She smiled up at him. "And I learned some very interesting things about our neighbors here in Baxter."

"Like what?"

"These cases are only the ones that made it to district court or superior court in Bangor. No parking tickets or anything like that. More than two hundred cases in the past two years."

"Wow. And Baxter only has what — five hundred residents?"

"Something like that."

"So 40 percent of all Baxter residents committed a crime in the last two years?"

Emily smiled ruefully. "Well, no. Thirty of the counts belong to Rocky Vigue. His spree last year."

"Oh, right." Nate flipped through the pages, frowning. "I suppose Mr. Derbin's murder is in here, too."

"Yes. But some of the names that turned up really surprised me. Were you aware that Erland Wilcox, who has the cottage right next to the Vigues' on the island, was summoned last year for failing to register his pickup?"

Nate eyed her cautiously. "Uh, no. I was not aware of that."

"And do you remember Jenna Marston?"

"No. Who's she?"

"One of the girls who worked for Raven last summer at the Vital Women Retreat Center."

"Oh, Jenna." Nate's face lit up.

Emily scowled at him. "Yeah, Jenna. You don't have to look so happy about remembering her."

He chuckled. "What about her?"

"The state police stopped her in August for driving under the influence."

"Of what?"

"Who knows?" Emily gave a half shrug. "She got a two-hundred-dollar fine. Anyway, a lot of people we know have police records."

Nate laid the papers down on the coffee table. "Emily, just because someone got a traffic ticket doesn't mean he would break into Lakeview Lodge in the middle of the night."

She grimaced. "I know. I'm just saying, it might have been someone Jeff knew, and who knew his habits. Somebody who knew his entire staff wouldn't be there for a couple of nights."

Nate squinted at the sheaf of printouts

but didn't pick them up. "So, how many thieves did you find?"

"Two."

"Two?"

"Yeah. Rocky and a woman from Aswontee who drove off without paying for her gas at the filling station last summer."

"Oh, she's a hard-core thief, then."

Emily punched his shoulder. "All right, laugh at me. I just want to help Jeff find out who did this so it won't happen again."

"I know your intentions are good, but . . ." Nate smiled. "You don't seriously think it was Rocky who jumped out that library window, do you? Because I'm not sure he could fit through the window frame, and I know he can't move very fast."

She sighed. "No, I don't think it was Rocky. Although I wouldn't have pegged him for the stealing he did last year, either."

"It could be someone from Aswontee or some other town."

"Yeah, it could be. But it could be someone right here in Baxter, too."

Nate nodded slowly, his eyes focusing on the far wall. "I suppose you're right, but I still think you should give the authorities time to investigate and see if they come up with anything."

Emily was a little disappointed at his lack

of enthusiasm, but she also knew he was now very conscious of going through the proper channels in legal matters. "Okay," she said.

He leaned over and kissed her cheek. Emily couldn't resist grinning and ruffling his shiny, dark hair. "Hey, I almost forgot. Mom wants us for Christmas. Is that okay?"

"Of course it's okay. I'd love to go down with you."

"You didn't make plans with your mother?" she asked.

"Nope. We don't usually do a big Christmas anymore. And I'm sure she'll have a lot going on at church."

"Oh good. I really miss Mom's cooking."

"Who cooks here?"

"Neither of us very often," Emily admitted, a little embarrassed. "Felicia doesn't like to, and I'm usually so busy."

"Well then, some home cooking is definitely in order for Christmas. Actually, I'm starving right now. Do you want to go out for something?"

"We have to," said Emily. "All we have is Cheerios."

Three weeks later, Emily hefted a stack of books onto the long oak table at the Maine Historical Society in Portland. They'd spent two days with Emily's mother for the holidays and had decided to stop at the research library before going home. Nate was already poring over a large hardback on the history of the town of Baxter.

"Find anything?" she asked, sitting down beside him.

"Not yet. This book mentions the lodge, but it doesn't talk about the treasure at all. What have you got?"

"A couple of town records, and even better, a book on the Eberhardt family in Maine."

His dark eyebrows shot up. "Where did you find that?"

"I told one of the librarians what we're looking for, and she recognized the name. It was in the stacks with other family histories. It makes me wonder if they have any old books on our ancestors."

"Yeah, maybe I'll check the stacks for books on the Holman clan when we're done with this. Grandma Holman always told us she was a Mayflower descendant, but she'd never documented it."

"That's neat." Emily began to skim through the table of contents, looking for anything related to the lodge. Her eyes soon fell on the name Alexander Eberhardt. "I think I've got something!"

Nate leaned in closer to look at the book as she flipped to the chapter about the original owner of the lodge. He scooted his chair nearer to hers, and they read silently until Emily whispered, "A missing fortune in silver certificates."

"Wow. So it was in paper bills."

"I was picturing gold for some reason."

"Me, too," said Nate. "Like buried pirate treasure."

"Mmm, yeah." Emily ran a finger down the page. "That confirms the legend, anyway, but there's not really anything else here. Let's check the town records."

Nate and Emily each took one of the red cloth-bound books from the stack and began to look for more information.

"Here's something about the Pineknoll Lumber Company buying land from an Eberhardt," Nate said.

Emily looked up from her book. "That's gotta be him. What else?"

Nate read further. "It says Eberhardt sold the bunkhouse and all the land to this other logging company, and then a few years later it changed hands again. Those owners subdivided it and sold the buildings and approximately one hundred acres of the land to Elisha Lewis in 1930."

Emily sat up straighter. "That's Jeff's

grandfather." An idea flashed into her mind, and she touched Nate's arm. "Let's stop at the county courthouse in Bangor on the way to Baxter and see if they have Mr. Lewis's will on file."

"Now, that's a thought. Do you want to leave now? I'll save Grandma Holman for another day."

Three hours later, Emily emerged from the Penobscot County Courthouse and took the steps two at a time. Nate waited for her in the SUV in front of the old, pillared red-brick building.

"I got a copy." She climbed in with the sheaf of papers in hand. The warm air in the vehicle felt good after her brief moments in the biting cold atmosphere that promised snow. "Sorry I took so long. I skimmed over it so I could brief you while you drive and you wouldn't have to have the light on in here."

"Good thinking," said Nate as he started the engine and put it into gear. "If we'd gotten here any later, the courthouse would have been closed." He flipped the lights on, although it was only a quarter to five. Maine's long December nights came early.

"The will was hard to read because it was handwritten in swirly, old-fashioned script."

Nate laughed. "I'm glad we don't have to

write like that nowadays. So, what's the scoop?"

"The plot thickens. It would seem the lodge and property were bequeathed to Jeff's father, but get this — Elisha Lewis's will also states that if the missing money is ever found on his property, it will be divided equally among all his living descendants. Nate, I'm not even sure that's enforceable."

He shrugged slightly. "I don't know."

"I guess I could call Mom's lawyer and ask. I'll do that sometime this week. I'm intrigued by this whole thing. I keep wondering what happened to the money."

"Yeah," Nate agreed. "Someone had to have taken or hidden it."

"I'm going to see what I can find out before this weekend, and then we can talk about it when you come up. Oh, and we need to choose the wedding invitations."

"No pink," said Nate.

She swatted him playfully with the papers. "Don't be silly. I wouldn't get pink ones."

"Whatever colors you want, Em." His smile told her that he was sincere and contented. She settled back in the seat, feeling blessed beyond her expectations.

Saturday afternoon found the two of them sitting at the kitchen table in Nate's mother's old house by the marina, going over invitation catalogs and revising their guest list. As excited as Emily was about her upcoming wedding, her mind kept straying back to the lost fortune.

"What do you think Jeff would do with the money if he found it?"

Nate looked up from the sample invitation he'd been scrutinizing. "My guess is he'd put it toward the renovations on the lodge."

"Imagine the publicity. The headlines. LUMBER BARON'S LOST TREASURE FOUND."

"I bet the lodge would be booked years in advance," said Nate. "A story like that would bring people from all over the country."

"Absolutely."

"Jeff could build that indoor swimming pool."

She chuckled. "I'm glad the attorney said Elisha Lewis's will isn't enforceable. That could cause all kinds of problems. But it was the way I thought it would be. A person can't bequeath something he's not sure exists."

"Right. If you could do that, can you imagine how it would tie up the courts?"

"Of course, the money probably won't

turn up. But I hope it does someday." She lapsed into thought, wondering where old Eberhardt could have hidden that cash. Her recent trip to the Bangor Public Library hadn't turned up any new information.

"I really think someone made off with it." Nate pushed back his chair and went to the counter to refill his coffee mug. "You know, we really haven't talked about it, but do you think you'd want to live here after we get married? I know you want to keep spending summers at the cottage on Grand Cat, but we have to stay somewhere in the winter, too."

"I thought you and your mom were going to sell the marina."

"We've talked about it some. But we don't necessarily have to sell the house with it." His cell phone rang, and he grabbed it off the counter and peered at the screen. "It's Jeff."

Emily dog-eared the catalog page for the invitation Nate had seemed to like the most. It was hard to tell, since he wasn't exactly enthusiastic about any of them. She wanted to include him in the wedding planning, but the truth was becoming evident: Nate would just as soon let her handle the minutia.

"Wow," he said into the phone. "What

happened?" He shot Emily a worried glance.

She felt a tingle go up her spine. What was wrong? Several unpleasant possibilities flashed across her mind as she waited for him to say more.

"Don't touch anything," he told Jeff. "Just wait for the police."

Emily bit her lip, barely able to keep quiet.

At last he said good-bye and closed his phone. "Em . . ."

"What's going on?"

He reached for her hand. "You remember Robert MacBriarty, the guy who gave us a tour while we were at the lodge?"

"Yeah, I remember Mac." He was Jeff's top guide and seemed to know everything there was to know about the Maine woods. "I really enjoyed going out to the cabin with him at Thanksgiving. Did something happen to him?"

Nate drew in a breath. "He's been murdered."

5

"Jeff asked me to go over and be with him at the lodge when the police arrive," Nate said. "He's shook up, and he wants someone there who knows about police procedure."

"What happened?" Emily asked.

"I don't know. Jeff found Mac's body upstairs in his bedroom." Nate reached into his pocket for his car keys.

Emily jumped up and closed the wedding invitation catalog. "Take me with you."

How did he know she would say that? Probably because Emily had a nose for news unmatched in the sixteen counties of Maine. "Aw, Em, I don't know . . ."

"Please?"

He winced. "Are you speaking as a curious bystander or as a reporter for the *Journal*?"

"I'm speaking as your fiancée. We don't have much time together now that you're at the academy, and . . ." She sighed and shrugged. "Okay, all of the above. Look at it this way. If you don't take me, I'll come in my own car as a reporter who got a hot tip, and you'll have to repeat everything Jeff and the police tell you to me. This way, I get it firsthand, and we save gas."

Nate put both hands to his head. She was smart, and she was persistent. Add the silky, honey blond hair and huge blue eyes, and he didn't have a chance. She'd had her way in nearly everything she'd asked of him since kindergarten. "All right. Come on. But you have to stay out of the way."

"No problem!" She grabbed her down jacket and dashed ahead of him to his SUV, jumping into the passenger seat before he could get there to open the door for her. He rounded the vehicle and climbed in, telling himself he was nuts to take her. If his instructors at the criminal justice academy heard he'd taken a civilian to a crime scene, he'd never live it down.

"So, Jeff called the police?" Emily asked as he pulled out of the marina parking lot.

"They're on their way, but the dispatcher told him the nearest state trooper is about an hour away."

"Typical."

"Yeah." He turned his concentration on the gravel road. He was taking the corners a

74

little faster than he should. This would not be a good to time to meet a pulp truck.

When they arrived at the lodge, Jeff's pickup truck was parked out front. This time Emily stayed put, looking around at everything long enough for Nate to get out and circle to open her door.

"I should have grabbed my camera," she moaned as she stepped down.

Nate was glad she hadn't thought of it. He decided not to mention the digital camera in his cell phone. They mounted the steps, and he opened the front door. The furniture in the lobby was covered by white dust sheets.

"Jeff? It's me."

Jeff came from the hallway that led to the kitchen, carrying a can of coffee. "Nate, I'm glad you're here. I was just starting a fresh pot of coffee. Come on back." He halted his steps when he saw Emily. "Oh, hi." Jeff arched his eyebrows at Nate.

"We were picking out wedding invitations when you called," Nate said with a half shrug.

Jeff nodded as if he understood. "Well, come on back to the kitchen. I don't think we should go upstairs until the cops get here, do you?"

"Probably best not to," Nate agreed.

"That is, as long as there's no one else up there . . ."

"There's not."

"And as long as you're sure he's dead. There's nothing we can do for him?"

"Definitely not." Jeff glanced at Emily and lowered his voice. "He's getting all stiff, Nate." He shuddered.

Nate inhaled deeply, recalling the lecture he'd recently heard about estimating time of death. But he was here in an unofficial capacity. The medical examiner would tend to that. "Okay, bring on the coffee."

They stepped over piles of lumber and drop cloths and followed Jeff down the hall. The kitchen was in even greater chaos.

"Sorry about the mess." Jeff went to the one spot on the counter not covered in plastic and scooped coffee into the hopper of a coffeemaker. "The electricians have been working on the wiring, and they had to tear out some walls. The contractor is supposed to start remodeling the kitchen on Monday, but the wiring's only half done. We're putting in heavier appliances, so we need heavier gauge wire and about a dozen more outlets for all Lucille's gadgets. I just hope we get finished in time to open by April first for fishing season."

"So, what happened to Mac?" Emily asked.

Nate frowned at her behind Jeff's back, but she only shrugged. Not that he wasn't curious, too, but he didn't want to push Jeff if he didn't want to talk about it until the police arrived.

Jeff pushed the button on the coffeemaker and turned toward them, leaning back against the counter. "I wish I knew. There's quite a lot of blood, but I admit that I got out of there as soon as I was sure he was dead. I didn't really look too close."

Nate caught Emily's glance. This news definitely raised the stakes in Emily's book, he could see. His own adrenaline surged. Six months ago they'd gladly helped in the resolution of Henry Derbin's murder and seen the case put away. Nate knew Emily would never be happy that someone had died, but she loved to work puzzles, and she seemed adept at solving crimes, if last summer was any indication.

"Mac went down to Massachusetts over Christmas to see his kids," Jeff told them. "But he and Shannon — that's his ex — aren't on very good terms, and he called a few days ago and asked if he could come back early. Shannon was driving him nuts. I told him he could, as long as he stayed out of the remodelers' way."

"So, all of the staff have been away since Christmas?" Nate asked.

"Yeah. I gave them all an extended leave while the work is being done. I've been here alone since last Friday. Until Mac came back Thursday night, that is."

The coffee filled the carafe, and Jeff took three mugs from a cupboard.

"When was the last time you saw him alive?" Nate asked, and Emily flashed him an approving smile.

"Last night. He'd been out ice fishing on the lake all day, and he came in around suppertime. We ate a sandwich together in the dining room and then took our coffee into the library and talked for a while. Mac went up to his room around nine. I read for a while and went to bed."

"So, is Mac's room on the second floor?" Emily asked as Jeff poured their mugs full.

"No, he's in the staff quarters on the third floor. He's stayed here pretty much year-round since he and Shannon got divorced."

"When was that?" Nate asked. Then he immediately added, "Sorry. You'll just have to tell the police all of this when they get here."

"It's okay. I think it was a couple of years ago."

"So you guys were pretty close."

Jeff shrugged. "He's awfully quiet, but I'd say I probably know him as well as anyone." He grimaced and caught himself. "Knew him, that is."

"You didn't hear anything unusual in the night?" Emily asked.

"No. But my room is two stories below Mac's, and clear at the other end of the lodge."

"And you didn't see Mac all day today?"

"No. At first I thought it was funny he didn't come down for breakfast, but then I decided he must have beat me getting up and gone out early. When it got dark again and I still hadn't seen a sign of him, I went up and knocked on his door. That's when I found him. I checked for a pulse, but it was too late." Jeff sighed.

"The coffee's ready." Emily pulled him gently aside. "Why don't you two go sit down in the lobby so you'll be handy when the state police get here? I'll bring a tray."

Nate followed Jeff out into the front of the lodge. Jeff yanked dust covers off a sofa and an armchair and dropped them on the floor behind the sofa. Emily brought their steaming mugs in, and they all sat down. Nate couldn't help wishing he could dash up the stairs and take a look, and he could tell Emily was itching to do the same. She kept glancing over toward the steps. But Nate knew they shouldn't go into the room before the police arrived.

Jeff ran a hand through his dark hair. "Man, I'd better call my brother and sister after the cops leave. I don't want them hearing about this on the news tonight."

"Probably best to break it to them yourself." Emily sipped her coffee.

"I suppose the cops will notify Mac's exwife."

"Yes, that's part of the job," Nate said. "Did you touch anything in Mac's room besides the body?"

Jeff shook his head. "Nothing. I came down here to use the phone. They're sending a detective Blakeney. Isn't he the one who investigated the Derbin murder last summer?"

"Yeah." Nate glanced at Emily. She had gotten under Blakeney's skin at times but had eventually earned his respect.

"Maybe we could pray about this while we wait," Emily suggested.

Jeff threw Nate a guarded glance. "Well, sure. I mean, if you want to."

Nate offered a brief prayer for wisdom, for Mac's family, and for a speedy resolution to the questions surrounding the guide's death. As he said "Amen," they heard tires crunch on the snowy driveway, and a moment later Jeff opened the lodge door to a uniformed man.

"Gary!" Nate stepped forward and greeted his cousin, Gary Taylor, who was in his third year as a Maine state trooper.

"Well, hi, Nate. Hi, Emily." Gary turned back to Jeff. "I'm sorry to hear about this. State Police Detective Blakeney is on his way, and he'll be in charge of the investigation, but he may be another hour getting here. He was on a call down in Newport when you phoned dispatch."

"Can you do anything, or do you have to wait for him?" Jeff asked.

"I can make a preliminary examination of the scene."

"Good." Jeff gave Gary a quick recap of events leading to his discovery of the body then said, "I'll take you up to Mac's room whenever you're ready."

Gary looked at Nate. "You're well into your training at the academy. Do you want to watch?"

"I'd love to," Nate said. "You wouldn't mind?"

Emily bounced on her toes beside him but kept quiet.

Gary grinned. "I don't suppose I can keep

Miss Gray, the ace reporter, down here if you go up. How about if you all stay in the hallway, and I'll be the only one who actually enters the room?"

With this agreement in place, they all mounted the two flights of stairs, and Jeff led them to the door of Robert MacBriarty's room.

Gary shined a flashlight across the bare floor and the throw rug before he entered the room.

"See that over there?"

Nate leaned around the doorjamb and followed the beam of Gary's flashlight.

"Looks like blood on the floor."

"Yeah." Gary cautiously approached the bed on the side away from the stained floor. From his position in the doorway, Nate saw mostly quilts on the bed, with a dark stain spreading from the lump that was the body. He could also see Mac's dark hair against the white of the pillowcase. Gary lifted the quilt by a corner and stared down at the body.

"We've put in a call for the medical examiner," he said, turning his head to address the three in the doorway, "but he may not be able to get here until morning."

"You mean I'll have to have him here all night?" Jeff nodded toward the body.

Gary shrugged. "We'll see. MacBriarty is definitely dead. I can't tell you how it happened, but definitely trauma. Seems to have bled a lot from his chest, but I can't tell what type of wound. The ME will have to tell us for certain."

"Is there a bullet hole in the quilt or anything like that?" Emily asked.

"Not that I can see. I don't want to disturb anything, but I'll tell you right now what seems to be missing."

"The weapon," Nate said immediately.

Gary nodded and lowered the quilt.

6

"You're treating this as a homicide, right?" Emily asked. Last summer she and Nate had discovered Henry Derbin's body on Grand Cat Island. At first, they'd wondered if the old man's death was an accident, but the evidence pointed to foul play. In this new case, it seemed more obvious.

"I think we can rule out suicide," Gary said. "No weapon close to the body. And an accident's also highly unlikely."

So that meant murder. Emily's spine prickled with excitement. She found Nate's hand, and he squeezed hers back. She felt a twinge of guilt but shook it off. Mysteries attracted her. The fact that the victim was someone she knew slightly didn't change that.

Gary stepped into the hallway and took a pen and a small writing tablet from his pocket. He stood for a minute jotting notes and sketching a diagram of the room.

"Okay, we'll need information from you," he said, pointing at Jeff with the pencil. "Names of everyone who's got access here. Staff, guests, friends, family."

"There are only two sets of keys to the front and back doors," said Jeff.

"Who has those?"

"I have one set, and my cook, Lucille, has the other."

Gary made a note. "Lucille's last name?"

"Robbins," said Jeff. He let out a long, deep breath.

Gary edged farther into the hallway. Emily backed against the wall to allow him more space.

Nate asked, "Would you like us to leave while you talk to Jeff?"

"No, it's fine. I like having another perspective," Gary replied. He clapped Nate on the shoulder.

Emily was glad he didn't seem to mind their being around. While Gary continued his questioning, she took mental notes. She'd decided it would be pushing it to take her notebook upstairs with her, and she wasn't about to ask Gary if she could borrow paper. She'd just have to remember the details.

"Who else works here?" Gary asked, positioning himself in front of the doorway to Mac's bedroom. "Kitchen help? Other guides?"

"Besides Lucille, in the kitchen there are Carrie Hayes and Michelle Keith. Carrie lives in Baxter and comes in most days to help Lucille with the cooking when we're open for guests."

Gary nodded. "And Ms. Keith?"

"She's part-time, weekends mainly, though she works full-time in the summer. She teaches kindergarten in Aswontee."

Jeff went on to name two of the other hunting guides he employed regularly, Sam Pottle and Royce Fairbanks, as well as the chambermaids, sisters Sarah and Virginia Walsh. Lisa Cookson acted as desk clerk but filled in as waitress or maid as needed. She usually stayed at the lodge during the summer and the peak hunting season. Gary took down all their names.

The lodge staff was larger than Emily had realized. That meant there were many people who had known and worked with Mac on a regular basis and might know things about him that would suggest a motive. Her mind filled with her own questions, and she had to force herself to listen.

She glanced at Nate, and he offered her a hesitant half smile. She knew he was curious, too, and that when they were alone

86

again they'd do some speculating of their own.

"How about contractors? Who's doing the renovations?"

"I've got a general contractor, a plumber, an electrician. They've all got helpers." Jeff started to list the companies at work on his renovation projects, but a loud knocking sounded at the front door.

"That's probably Blakeney," said Gary.

Nate turned toward the stairs. "I'll go."

"No, I'd better," said Gary. "Don't move." He took off down the stairs.

Jeff sighed. "I just can't believe this is happening. I mean . . . Mac! And I was right here."

Emily thought he looked pale. "Can I get you some coffee or something? Maybe you should sit down."

A man's loud voice reached them easily from two stories below. "What did you let them upstairs for?"

Emily grimaced. She would have recognized Blakeney's voice anywhere.

Gary's voice was softer, and she couldn't make out his response.

"Should we go down?" she whispered.

"It's a crime scene," came Blakeney's voice again, "not a picnic. Who does that girl think she is, Nancy Drew?"

"Yeah, I think we should go down," Nate said.

Emily felt her face flame. "I didn't think it was a big deal if I'm here for the press. Will Gary get in trouble?"

"I hope not." Nate motioned for Jeff to go first; then Emily followed him down the stairs with Nate close behind.

Blakeney rounded on them immediately. "The three of you, over there," he thundered, swinging his whole arm and pointing toward the seating area in the lobby. "And stay there until I'm through upstairs."

Nope, he hasn't changed a bit, Emily thought. *And here I was prepared to greet him politely.*

Jeff stood by the far wall, staring out a window as Gary and the detective went upstairs to Mac's room.

Emily took a seat on the sofa. Anger boiled inside her, though she knew Blakeney had a right to be upset if he felt they were interfering with police procedure. But she thought he could have been nicer about it. Surely veteran officers like Blakeney had undergone training in dealing with civilians at crime scenes. She hoped Gary wouldn't suffer consequences for her eager curiosity.

Nate sat down beside her and put an arm around her shoulders. After a few minutes, she said softly, "I'm getting my notebook. No matter what Blakeney says, I'm covering this story, and I need to write down the details while they're fresh in my mind." She retrieved the small notebook she always carried in her purse. After a few minutes, Nate began to talk quietly with her, going over what they had seen. Jeff slumped in an armchair near the windows and didn't speak for a long time. Then he got up and paced slowly from the dining room doorway to the lobby windows and back, his hands shoved deep in his pockets.

After half an hour, the officers came down the stairs. Blakeney stood to one side as he made a call on his radio.

"We're sending for a mobile crime lab," Gary told them as he walked across the lobby to stand near them. He paused, twirling his pen between his thumb and fingers. "Jeff, I'm going to need the rest of those names now. Blakeney will question you when he's through with the call."

Emily watched as Jeff turned away from the window to face the room again. His face was white, and his normally smiling mouth drooped. Emily thought he looked unwell, and she wished she could do something to help him.

"Have a seat." Gary nodded toward the

armchair.

Jeff sat down again, and Gary took another chair close by. With prompting, Jeff told Gary that Pine Tree Builders had sent a couple of men over to do the drywall. He was unsure of their last names, but Gary said they could easily check up on it. Some people from Oliver Electric were doing the rewiring, and Jeff mentioned a plumber who was a friend of his.

Blakeney cursed audibly from the hallway that led to the kitchen.

"What's up?" Gary called.

Blakeney swaggered into the room, quickly regaining composure. "The mobile crime lab can't get here until tomorrow morning," he said. "They're working another case in Lewiston. It will take them hours to assemble the right personnel and restock their gear and get up here."

Gary nodded. "Shall we tape off the scene?"

"Tape off the whole third floor and then look around outside. I'll finish here."

Gary went out to his car and returned with a roll of yellow plastic police-line tape. As he headed up the stairs with it, Blakeney turned his attention to Jeff.

"You discovered the body?" He approached Jeff's chair but did not sit down as Gary had done.

He was an intimidating figure, Emily thought, taller than Nate, and his dark hair and chiseled features only exaggerated his air of dominance. She couldn't blame Jeff for squirming a bit as Blakeney glowered down at him.

"Yes, officer," said Jeff. He went on to tell the story as he had told it to Gary, Nate, and Emily earlier.

The detective had Jeff recount the story again, asking frequent questions and sometimes asking him to repeat information. Did Blakeney consider Jeff the prime suspect? Emily shuddered at the thought.

Nate must have been thinking the same thing. His forehead wrinkled in concentration as he leaned forward to watch the interrogation unfold.

"Have you told anyone else about this yet?" Blakeney asked.

"No, sir. I called 911 then my friend Nate. I asked him to come wait with me."

"All right, we'll need the contact information for MacBriarty's next of kin."

"I have that information in my office. He has an ex-wife and children in Massachusetts, but I think he put down his brother as his emergency contact."

Blakeney went with Jeff to the office to

retrieve the information. As they emerged a few minutes later, Gary came down the stairs.

"I've taped it off." He looked at Jeff. "You won't be able to let anyone up there until we're through with the investigation."

Jeff nodded. "I've already given the staff an extended vacation until the remodeling is finished. I hope to reopen at the beginning of April, though."

"Well, you need to put your renovations on hold," said Blakeney. "I don't want those workmen in here now."

"That's fine," said Jeff. "Whatever you need."

"It's best if you don't stay here," Gary said. "Is there somewhere you could stay, Jeff, until the preliminary investigations are concluded?"

Nate cleared his throat. "You're welcome to stay with me. I have plenty of room."

Jeff shook his head. "No, I don't want to be a bother." He shrugged his shoulders. "I'll get a hotel room in Aswontee."

"I don't want you to do that." Blakeney's stern voice could be mistaken for nothing short of a warning.

Emily bit her lip as the blood rose in her cheeks and her heart beat faster. Aswontee was only fifteen miles away. Did Blakeney think Jeff was going to run?

"You'd better stick around town," the detective said. "Stay with Holman. We'll know where to find you if we need you."

"You'd be no trouble," Nate said quickly to Jeff.

"I suppose I have no other choice." Jeff rose from his chair. "I'll pack a bag."

Nate and Emily stood, too.

"Taylor, go with him," Blakeney said.

Emily stared at him, but Blakeney ignored her. Her mind raced. If the detective had evidence that Jeff was the killer, he would arrest him now, but he hadn't done that. Still, he was making sure Jeff stayed within easy reach. No one had illusions about the situation. Jeff was Suspect Numero Uno. Nate slid his arm around her waist but said nothing. They both watched as Gary followed Jeff toward his private quarters.

7

Nate stood over his kitchen stove with a spatula in his hand, watching the eggs in the frying pan. The yolks were almost perfect when the doorbell rang. He groaned and glanced toward the doorway, then back at the frying pan. Jeff sat at the kitchen table alternately yawning and sipping coffee while Nate got breakfast, but he stood when the chimes echoed through the old wood frame house at the lake's edge.

"Want me to get that?"

"Sure," Nate said. "If it's Emily, invite her in for some chow."

It took him only seconds to realize he was far off the mark. Detective Blakeney's deep voice reached him from two rooms away.

"Morning, Lewis. Just dropping by to tell you that you'll have to stay away from the lodge all day today."

Nate took the frying pan off the burner and shut the heat off. He went through the living room to the entry hall.

"Okay," Jeff said. "Uh . . . there's some food in the refrigerator at the lodge. If this is going to take a while, maybe someone should clean it out?"

"I'll let you know." Blakeney noticed Nate in the doorway and nodded. "Morning, Holman."

"Hi. Would you like some coffee?"

"No, I'm on my way out to the lodge. We expect the mobile crime lab within an hour, and we'll probably be busy out there all day."

Jeff cleared his throat. "Uh, if I'm allowed to ask, is the . . . uh . . . is Mac still out there?"

"No, Grebel's Mortuary in Aswontee picked the body up last night. They'll transport it for us to the medical examiner for an autopsy."

"Sure." Jeff ducked his head, and his face took on that ashen color he'd had last night.

"Has Mac's family been notified yet?" Nate asked.

"Yes, I reached his brother last night," Blakeney said. "He offered to tell the rest of the family, including the ex. But they know the body won't be released for a few days at least."

Nate looked over at Jeff, who rocked on

his feet as though he might keel over any second. Nate decided getting Blakeney out of the house was a priority.

"We plan to go to church this morning," he said. "I'll have my cell phone if you need to contact us."

Blakeney eyed Jeff for a moment then nodded. "All right. Just keep yourself available, Lewis. We'll let you know when you can go back to the lodge."

As the door closed behind the detective, Jeff's shoulders slumped. He turned slowly and grimaced at Nate.

"I guess it's pretty clear where I stand with him."

"Don't let it get you down," Nate said. "He has to look hard at you. After all, you were the only other person in the house with Mac. Except the killer, of course." Nate winced over his blunder and hurried on, "Come on, the eggs are ready. Let's eat and go over to Felicia's house. I usually pick Emily up on Sunday morning."

"Oh, I don't know as I'm up to going to church." Jeff smiled apologetically. "People are talking, you know?"

"Do I ever. But if you go to church with your chin up, they'll be more apt to come down on your side. You need support now, Jeff. The people of Baxter like you, and they'll want to help you any way they can. When this is over, you'll be glad you didn't shut yourself off from friends and neighbors."

Jeff sighed. "You're probably right. I didn't sleep very well, though. I mean, we both know Blakeney thinks I murdered Mac. That's rough."

Nate put his hand on Jeff's shoulder. "I don't think that. And I don't think Blakeney's ruled out other possibilities, either. But he wouldn't be doing his job if he didn't treat you like a suspect."

"Do you think he'll do a good investigation?"

Nate considered that for a moment. "Yeah, I do. He's good at his job. When Emily and I brought him some clues in the Derbin case, he acted a little standoffish, but he didn't ignore us. He'll take information any way he can get it, and he wants to know the truth. He's not out to get you unless you're guilty, which you're not."

"Thanks. I'll try to keep that in mind," Jeff said.

Nate cuffed him on the back. "Come on, I'm starved."

That afternoon Emily helped Nate's mother do the dishes after Sunday dinner. When the last plate was dried and put in the china cupboard, Connie Phillips smiled at her future daughter-in-law.

"I usually take a nap about now. Why don't you go join the fellows in the front room?"

Emily found Nate stretched out on the sofa near the fireplace, browsing a magazine, but he sat up quickly when she appeared and replaced the magazine on the coffee table.

"Where are Jeff and Pastor?" Emily asked, plopping down beside him.

"In Pastor's study." He moved in closer and slid his arm around her.

Emily leaned back and arched her eyebrows.

"This is good, right?"

"I think so. Jeff is really taking this thing with Mac hard. He's worried about Blakeney keeping him in the suspect bracket, too."

"That's to be expected, I guess, though it must be depressing for Jeff. I can't imagine how I'd feel if it were me . . . or you."

"Yeah. We got to talking about it, and Dad Phillips was giving Jeff some encouragement. He invited him into his study so he could show him some scripture."

Emily smiled and laid her head on Nate's

shoulder. "I'm glad he's ready to listen. This has been a big shock for Jeff. I had a hard time sleeping last night myself. My mind kept going back to the murder, so I just kept praying for Jeff."

"Me, too. I think several people in Baxter had insomnia last night."

"I wish we could be closer to the investigation." She sighed. "I can understand Blakeney not wanting me poking my nose in, but this would be great training for you — to see a murder investigation firsthand, up close, and —"

Nate bent to kiss her, and Emily stopped talking. She knew Nate was frustrated, too, and talking about it would only intensify those feelings. But kissing Nate — now, that would distract her from a lot of minor grievances. When he released her, she leaned against him in contentment. "I should have brought the catalog. We still haven't decided on the style for the invitations, and I need to get that order in."

Nate leaned back and said nothing for a long time.

"Honey?" Emily asked.

"Yeah?"

"You do want invitations, right?"

"Well, yeah." He shifted, and Emily looked up at him. He seemed to be fighting a frown unsuccessfully. "You know what would really make me happy?"

"What?"

He hesitated. "Okay, I'll just say it. Why don't you just pick out what you like? I know I won't hate it, and it would make everything so much easier."

Emily stared into those soft chocolate eyes for ten seconds, telling herself he really did care about her, the wedding, and their future together. It was only the froufrou details that annoyed him.

"Is that what you really want?"

"Well . . . I know you have great taste, and to be honest, I don't care if they have curlicues or flowers or starbursts. All I care about is our names together with the words holy matrimony, telling the world you're going to be my wife."

She smiled. "All right. You said the right thing. Actually, that's about the way I figured you felt. We don't have to do everything together. I'll pick one and place the order tomorrow."

His expression cleared as though she'd granted him a reprieve from a heavy sentence. "Thank you."

She twined her arms around his neck and kissed him again.

■ ■ ■ ■

The sun was setting over the frozen lake when Blakeney returned to the house beside the marina. Nate and Jeff had been home for an hour, and Nate was starting to think about making sandwiches for supper and wondering how they would get through the long evening. He invited the detective in and sat down with him and Jeff in the living room.

"All right, Lewis; here's where we are," Blakeney said. "The body is in Augusta, and the medical examiner will start the autopsy tomorrow morning. The crime scene team cataloged a lot of evidence at the lodge today, and they'll sort out what's relevant to the murder and what's not." He held out a piece of paper. "This is a receipt for a few items we took as evidence. If all goes well, you'll get them back later."

Jeff took the list and grimaced as he skimmed it. "If it's all the same to you, I don't need the bedding back."

Blakeney nodded. "Okay. And I've interviewed several members of the lodge staff today."

Jeff sat back and met his gaze. "Good. I'm glad you could get hold of them."

Blakeney stretched out his long legs. "Yeah, well, you might not be so happy when I tell you what one of them told me."

Apprehension clouded Jeff's face.

Blakeney went on, "One of the other guides, Royce Fairbanks . . ."

Jeff nodded.

"He said you and MacBriarty had a disagreement last fall. I made some inquiries after I talked to Fairbanks, and I learned that MacBriarty was arrested at the time."

Jeff shifted in his chair and cleared his throat, not quite looking at Blakeney. "That's right."

"You want to tell me about that?"

Jeff shot a look at Nate that he could only interpret as a plea for help. All he could do for him now was pray.

Lord, help Jeff. Keep him calm, and help him to be open with Blakeney.

Jeff drew a deep breath and nodded. "It was during the moose season. Mac took a party out moose hunting. There were four men from the Portland area. One held the permit, one was the alternate shooter, and the other two just came along for kicks."

Blakeney pulled out his notebook and wrote something down. "You have all their names on file, I assume?"

"Sure. At the lodge, in my office. At least

the permittee's name and address, and whichever one paid the bill. It was the Miller party. If you check the file cabinet beside my desk, you'll find a folder under *M* for Miller."

Blakeney nodded.

Jeff went on. "They came in from the hunt successful, and they were all celebrating. But later, one of the guests said that Mac shot his moose for him."

"What did you do?" the detective asked.

"I was shocked and disappointed in Mac. I thought it over for a few hours, but I knew what I had to do. I mean, if it got around that Lakeview Lodge's guides would do something like that . . ."

"So you turned him in?"

Jeff winced and shook his head. "I was going to. But I wanted to talk to him first. I'd just made up my mind to confront him when Sarah — she's one of the chambermaids — came in and told me a game warden was out front and wanted to speak to me. He said he'd had an anonymous tip and he was there to arrest Mac."

"But you didn't make the call."

"No. But I would have if Mac couldn't look me in the eye and tell me he didn't do it. I was ready to do what I had to. But the way it happened, I felt bad for Mac — I liked him. I wished I'd had a chance to talk things through with him first. But anyway, someone made the call. When someone other than the permit holder or the sub-permittee shoots the moose, that's a crime. We all know that. I couldn't let it happen on my property and under the auspices of my business."

Blakeney grunted and continued to write. "Who was the warden?"

"Uh . . . That guy from Orono . . . Jackson, I think?"

"I know him."

"He can tell you about it," Jeff said. "When Mac was released on bail the next day, he came back to the lodge. I had a long talk with him in my office. I suppose it may have escalated, and our voices may have become loud enough to be construed as an argument."

"So Mac was angry at you?"

"He thought I'd called the warden. I told him I didn't, but I also told him that if he ever pulled a stunt like that again, I'd have to fire him. As it was, I took him off guiding until after his court appearance. That put a cramp in our style, I'll tell you. We had more hunting parties than Royce and Sam could handle. I had to persuade a retired guide to take out a few parties for me, and I paid him royally for helping me out. Meanwhile, I kept Mac on maintenance. Afterward I wondered if maybe I should have fired him on the spot, but I cut him a break, you know? He's been with the lodge a long time — since before my dad died. As far as I know, he'd never done anything like that before."

"Had he gone to court yet?" Blakeney asked.

"Yeah. The case was dismissed for insufficient evidence."

"I thought he admitted it."

"Not in so many words. When I raked him over the coals, he acted pretty remorseful, but he never said he did it."

"Did he say he didn't?"

Jeff gulped and met the detective's steely eyes. "Well, no. But I've always liked Mac, so I gave him another chance."

"How was he after that?"

"Fine. Things were cordial between us. You know, I'm still not a hundred percent sure whether or not Mac shot that client's moose. But I figured if he didn't, he'd have defended himself. He didn't do that. He just let me rail at him, and he never complained about my taking him off duty."

Blakeney put his notebook away and stood. "All right, Lewis. You just hang in there and do what you're doing. In other words, stick around and be available when I want to talk to you again. I'll look into this hunting thing more closely."

"Can I go back to the lodge now?"

"Not yet."

Jeff slumped back in his chair.

Nate walked Blakeney out to the driveway. When they reached the unmarked police car, he ventured, "Sir, I'm sure Jeff is giving it to you straight."

Blakeney's granite gaze drilled into him. "If he's not, I'll find out. Just because he's your friend, Holman, don't think he's not capable of committing a crime. I understand you're in training at the academy. You know it's hard to stay objective in a case like this, but it's vital."

"Yes, sir, I understand. Oh, and Detective, did anyone tell you about the break-in at the lodge Thanksgiving night?"

Blakeney's eyes narrowed. "First I've heard of it."

"Well, sir, it's probably not related to this murder, but Emily and I were out there visiting Jeff that weekend, and no one else was there except the three of us. Someone broke in that night. Jeff heard him and scared him off."

"Did he call it in?"

"Yes. One of county sheriff's deputies responded. But nothing was taken, and in the six weeks since then, I don't think Jeff's heard any more about it."

"Probably nothing, but you never know. I'll look into it. Thanks, Holman."

After the detective was gone, Nate figured he should start supper, but he wasn't sure he could get Jeff to eat. His friend sat unmoving in the armchair, staring at the opposite wall.

"So, you want to go out, Jeff? We could get something to eat at the Lumberjack."

"No thanks. I'm still full from your mom's dinner."

Nate headed for the kitchen. Sooner or later they'd have to eat something. He opened the refrigerator and closed it again. Maybe Emily would come over and cook something. Yeah, right. Cooking was low on Emily's list of favorite pastimes. Sometimes he wondered what they would eat after they were married. She could cook, he knew. But she could also be content to go for days on sandwiches and takeout.

He heard a car drive in, so he went back to the living room and looked out the window. Gary was walking up to the front door. Nate went to meet him.

"Hey," Gary said. "I'm heading home for

107

the night. Did Blakeney come here?"

"Yeah, he just left," Nate said. "He didn't tell us much, just grilled Jeff about his relationship with Mac. Did you guys find anything today?"

Gary shrugged. "Maybe."

"Any murder weapon?" Nate asked. He would never have dared ask Blakeney, but after all, Gary was his cousin.

"No, but they impounded all of Jeff's guns and hunting knives."

Nate gritted his teeth. "I guess they have to, at least until the ME is done with the autopsy. Anything else you can tell me?"

Gary looked beyond Nate toward the interior of the house. "Where's Jeff?"

"In the living room."

Gary lowered his voice. "Well, just between you and me, I don't think they've got enough evidence to arrest him. Blakeney's working it. He's really pushing the crime lab to give this priority."

"Are they looking at other suspects besides Jeff?" Nate asked.

"Yeah. I mean, we're interviewing all the staff and those repairmen that were working out there, and Blakeney talked to the former Mrs. MacBriarty on the phone. We've got to verify that she stayed in Massachusetts this weekend. But the cops down there will help us with that."

"So there aren't any other suspects that really look good. That's what you're saying."

Gary shook his head. "Afraid not. Blakeney likes Jeff for it."

Nate's heart sank. "You said they took his knives?"

"Yeah. The preliminary word is MacBriarty was stabbed."

Gary declined his invitation to eat supper with them, which was just as well. Nate no longer felt like eating, either. When Gary left, he and Jeff sat in dejected silence for a few minutes. Nate thought of turning on the television, but during this hour all the stations he could receive without benefit of cable — a luxury unknown yet in Baxter — would carry news reports, and he thought that would only further discourage Jeff. All the stations must be broadcasting news of the murder.

His phone rang, and he answered it in the kitchen, happy for the diversion and even more so when Emily's cheerful voice rang in his ear.

"Hey, babe! I ordered those invitations. What do you think of that?"

He couldn't help grinning. "You ordered them online?"

"Yup. They should be here by next week."

"Great. Thanks for doing that, Em."

"How's Jeff?"

"Not good," Nate admitted. "Blakeney was here. He seems focused on Jeff as the most likely to crack and murder an employee."

"Oh, that makes me so mad!"

Nate winced and held the phone a bit farther from his ear.

Emily went on, "I mean, they should be giving Mac's ex-wife the third degree. What about her, hmm?"

"Well, he did say they're checking her whereabouts this weekend."

"Well, she probably didn't do it herself. She probably hired some hit man to drive up here and shoot Mac. Has Blakeney thought of that, I wonder?"

Nate suppressed a smile. "You could call him and suggest it. I'm sure he'd love your input."

"Oh, you think you're so funny!"

"Hey, I did learn unofficially that they think he was stabbed, but they haven't found a weapon yet."

"Yeah? Huh. I'll have to snag an update from Blakeney tomorrow morning. Maybe we could squeeze it into Tuesday's *Journal*."

"Sure," Nate said.

"I heard something else," she told him. "It may just be gossip."

"What's that?"

"Felicia and I went over to the Lumberjack for supper —"

"I tried to get Jeff to go over there, and he didn't want to. Said he didn't feel like eating."

"Yeah, well, everybody in town is talking about this thing. I don't know that I blame him for not wanting to go out in public much. But anyway, Jon Woods told us he'd heard that another guide — not one who works for Jeff, but some independent outfitter — was mad at Mac for pirating some of his best-paying clients."

"Do you think it's true?" Nate asked.

"I don't know, but it might force the police to look at someone other than Jeff if we point them to someone with a motive. If Blakeney's nice and gives me a good interview for the *Journal,* I just might hand him the other guide's name."

8

"So, you think there was bad blood between MacBriarty and this Ormond Hill?"

"Well, it's only a rumor that I heard, Detective, as I said." Emily watched Blakeney scratch the information into his notebook on Monday morning. She wondered if he ever smiled. "I don't want to get anyone in trouble, but it seemed to me like something you should know."

Blakeney's gray eyes drilled into her again. "And you heard this from Jonathan Woods, over at the garage?"

"Yes. I'm sure he can tell you more about it than I can."

"All right, I'll see what I can find out." He slid the notebook into his pocket.

Emily stood. "Thank you for the information."

"You're welcome. I'll look for the article in tomorrow's *Journal.* And you'd better not misquote me." He walked across the small room and went out, letting in a blast of frigid air.

Emily sighed with relief as the door to the newspaper office closed and Detective Blakeney disappeared. Despite her interest in the story, Blakeney was a difficult interviewee. She could almost feel the atmosphere in the office relax now that he was gone.

"All done?" Felicia poked her head in through the doorway of the small room full of file cabinets they referred to as the morgue. "Boy, he's a beast. Did you hear the way he spat every time he said Jeff's name?"

"Yes," said Emily. "I think I felt it a couple times, too." She wrinkled her nose.

"Eew. And did I hear him tell you not to interfere with police procedure?"

"It's nothing I haven't heard before." Emily winked. "Anyway, I think I need time to let my head clear before I write my article." She pushed her chair back, scooped up her notebook, and started for the door. "I'm off to Augusta."

"Visiting Nate?" Felicia batted her eyelashes.

"Nope, he's still here in town. They have another week for their Christmas break from the academy. This is strictly a research jaunt."

"Aha!" said Felicia. "Sticking your nose where it doesn't belong?"

Emily shrugged her shoulders with exaggeration. "Blakeney never said not to interfere with library business."

Felicia nodded. "That's why I like having you at the *Journal.*"

At the Maine State Archives, Emily went straight to the vital records. If she couldn't poke around in the MacBriarty case, she'd go back to the story of the lumber baron's treasure. She hoped to find out more about André, the lumberjack who drove Alexander Eberhardt to Bangor on his fateful trip so many years ago. She had very little to go on, without even a last name, and her search for information had so far proved fruitless. Half an hour's searching through the ledgers and box files on the shelves brought her no closer to the data she wanted. In frustration, she went to the circulation desk to ask for some help.

"That's a tough one," said the petite, red-haired woman. "I'm new here. But our chief archivist is in the office. Would you like me to get him?"

"Please," Emily said eagerly. "This is really

important, and I'm out of ideas."

When the archivist came out of the office, Emily explained the situation to him.

"Let me see what I can find," he said. "We have some microform materials that may be of use to you."

A few minutes later, Emily carried a stack of microfilm reels to a reader and threaded the first tape through the feeder. The first spool consisted of several editions of an obsolete newspaper covering the area of Baxter and several other small townships. The weekly editions mainly offered colorful yarns about the lumber camps, family farms, and church picnics.

While she skimmed these for names, the archivist approached with a couple of books. "I've found something in the vital records you may have overlooked. There was an André Pushard mentioned, and another source confirms his working for Eberhardt."

Emily spent the next two hours scanning microfilm and poring over books that the archivist brought to her. Putting the clues together piece by piece, she learned that Pushard's home town was St. Aurelie, Quebec, not far from the Maine border. She requested help in researching family history in Quebec. By midafternoon, she realized she was running short on time and decided to copy some of the records to take back with her.

She was standing over the copier when the archivist returned again. "I've got an old journal here. It was kept by a man who lived in Brewer. He worked for a couple of years as a clerk for Alexander Eberhardt, and it has some entries I believe are related to Eberhardt's business."

"Oh, thank you!" said Emily. "Just add it to my stack." She motioned to the books she had piled on a chair beside the copier.

"The problem is, the diary is in French, and we don't have a translation. But there's a written description of the book in our index that tells when he worked for Eberhardt, so I thought there could be something pertinent."

"Okay," said Emily. "If it's not too many pages, I'll copy it and take it with me. At this point, I'll take anything I can get."

With her folder of papers, she left the archives around four o'clock. After a two-hour drive, she arrived home eager to dive into the material, dig out her college French dictionary, and see what else she could learn. She sighed deeply as she let her folder and notebook drop to the tabletop in Felicia's kitchen.

"Something wrong?" Felicia was peering

into the refrigerator with a look of expectation, as if hoping her left-over Chinese food would turn into a chocolate cake. "I seriously need to shop."

"I'm just eager to work on some stuff I brought home from the archives, but I need to write up my interview with Detective Blakeney first."

"You bet your boots," said Felicia, closing the fridge. "I need that tomorrow."

"It won't take me long. But I'm not feeling motivated."

Felicia pondered for a moment. "I could threaten to fire you."

Emily laughed. "Okay, okay. I'm on it."

A sudden crackling sound was followed by a clear voice saying, "PSD 7, what's your twenty?"

Emily stared at Felicia. "You brought the police-band radio home from the office?"

Felicia laughed. "No, I bought another one. Don't you want to be able to monitor your sweetie's movements when he starts working for the sheriff's department?"

Emily winced and walked over to the counter where the new radio set was perched between the coffeemaker and the toaster. "I'm not so sure that's a good idea. It almost seems like spying."

"Aw, come on. We eavesdrop on the cops

all the time at the office. But sometimes on the weekend we miss out on a story because we don't hear about it until Monday."

"Or until we read the *Bangor Daily*," Emily said with a chuckle.

"Just because we're a biweekly doesn't mean we have to be behind the game." Felicia shrugged. "Besides, if Nate's going into a high-risk situation, don't you want to know about it?"

"Well . . ."

"You don't want to be the last person to get the call, do you? I know you don't."

"I suppose." Emily took up her notebook and started for the living room. Halfway there, she turned around. "Felicia?"

"Yeah?" She had the refrigerator open again but turned to peer at Emily over her glasses.

"When I'm done, you wanna go out for pizza?"

"You bet your boots."

Nate pulled into the dirt driveway of the lodge and parked beneath one of the large cedar trees. "Here we are."

"Thanks for putting me up," said Jeff. "It was a big help."

"No problem. It was the least I could do."

They got out of the SUV and started

toward the front porch.

"Can you get things moving again with the contractors now?" Nate asked as he followed Jeff inside.

"Detective Blakeney said the police may be in and out for follow-up questioning, but it seems I'm pretty much free to do whatever I want now with the renovations."

"That's a relief. You've had quite a delay already, and that can't be good for business."

"Yeah. I should still be able to open on schedule for the beginning of fishing season. It's just going to be a lot of work."

Inside, Jeff walked to the bottom of the stairs and looked up. "You know, I still keep hoping this is all a dream."

Nate leaned against the newel post, unsure of what to say.

"I wish I knew why it happened here," Jeff went on. "Someone was mad at Mac and decided to kill him. But why at my lodge? I've got these questions in my mind I can't get away from."

"Yeah, I know," said Nate. "What about your brother and sister? Have you contacted them? This might be a good time to get some support from your family."

Jeff looked over the empty lobby with a sigh. "I called them that first night. They were both sympathetic, but they have their own lives. It's not something that directly impacts them, you know."

"But still . . ."

"Since Mom and Dad died, we haven't been close. We talk once in a while, but . . ."

Nate put a hand on Jeff's shoulder. "Are you sure you shouldn't take some time off?"

"No," said Jeff. "I can't go away, anyhow. There's too much to be done, and I've already waited too long."

"Okay," Nate said. "Hey, I know Blakeney can be a bit tough, but he's an expert at what he does, and I'm sure things will get cleared up as soon as possible."

"Thanks, Nate."

In early February, Emily made her weekly call to Blakeney. The state police dispatcher put her on hold while she tried to patch the call through. Emily pulled a pocket calculator from her desk drawer. Might as well get a jump on balancing her checkbook while she waited.

The lack of progress on the MacBriarty case would have been laughable if the topic weren't so serious. Emily hated to even ask for information anymore. Week after week, Blakeney gave her the same line: "There's nothing I can tell you at this time, but we're working on it."

Meanwhile she and Felicia had kept busy covering town government, school events, fires, accidents, crime — anything deemed newsworthy within a twenty-five-mile radius of Baxter. The paper kept the two of them running like marathoners. Charlie Benton, who handled all the ads for the *Journal,* had threatened to quit if Felicia didn't hire someone to help him. The good news was that the paper now turned a solid profit.

"Yes, Miss Gray?" Blakeney's gravelly voice said in her ear.

Emily shoved her bank statement and calculator aside, uncovering her notebook.

"Hello, Detective. I wondered if there's anything new on the MacBriarty murder."

"I'm afraid not."

Emily winced. "Surely your department has processed all the evidence you collected."

"We have."

"Are you saying it hasn't led to any leads for you to follow?"

"I didn't say that. Don't put words in my mouth."

She felt her cheeks redden, even though he couldn't see her. "That wasn't my intention, sir. But if you don't give me anything quotable . . ."

"Ha! All you reporters care about is a snappy quote. Well, quote this: We have a suspect. We hope to make an arrest eventually but not yet."

"I don't understand what's taking so long," Emily said. "Could you explain to me what is happening that may lead to an arrest?"

Blakeney swore, and she flinched.

"Look, Miss Gray, we don't like to make an arrest until we're sure we have enough evidence to convict the suspect. If we make our move too soon, the district attorney will say we don't have a case, and we have to let the suspect go. It's a waste of taxpayers' money. The folks in Augusta don't like it when that happens."

"Oh, I understand that, sir, but . . ."

"But what?"

"Well, we both know that Jeff Lewis is your main suspect in this case —"

"Did I say that?" Blakeney snapped.

"Well, no, not in so many words."

"That's right. And if you were to print something like that . . ."

"I won't. Not until you tell me to."

"Good. Anything else? Because I've got a robbery in Wittapitlock to investigate. Do you mind?"

"No, sir." She hung up and slumped in

her chair.

"Get bitten by the big, bad Blakeney?" Felicia asked from across the room.

"Yup. I guess the upside is that they don't have a shred of evidence against Jeff Lewis."

"Yeah, but we can't print that."

"So I've been told."

"Hmm." Felicia wiggled her eyebrows. "Maybe we could print a list of all the citizens in Baxter against whom Blakeney has no evidence and put Jeff's name at the top."

Emily laughed. "Yeah, right."

Felicia shrugged. "Oh, well. We've still got holes on pages three and four for Friday's edition. Were you going to do that profile of the guy who drives the town snowplow?"

"Sure," Emily said without enthusiasm. "And you can call the weatherman at the TV station in Bangor for our weekly report on conditions for skiing and ice fishing. Do you want my usual weekly two-inch non-story on the MacBriarty case?"

"People will ask if you don't write it."

Emily picked up her pen with a scowl. "We should just put a little box down on the corner of page one every Friday that says, 'Ditto on the MacBriarty case.' "

By the end of February, Emily was so

starved for news of the investigation that she worked up her nerve to call the county sheriff's office and ask for Deputy Russell Young. He called her back an hour later.

"May I help you, Miss Gray?"

Emily gulped and put a smile in her voice. "Hi. I don't know if you remember me, but I was at Lakeview Lodge with my fiancé, Nate Holman, the night you responded to a report of a break-in last Thanksgiving."

"I remember," Young said.

"Oh. Good."

"What can I do for you?"

"Well, it's about the pocketknife you took away from the lodge that night . . . the one the intruder dropped."

"We logged it as evidence."

"You still have it, then?"

After a pause, Young said, "Actually, the state police asked us to transfer that knife to them in January."

Emily drew in a careful breath. So Blakeney thought there might be a connection between the break-in and Mac's murder more than a month later.

"Do you know something about the knife?" Young asked.

"Me? No. To be honest, I work for the *Baxter Journal,* and I was hoping I could see the knife. Just as part of some research I'm doing."

"Research about the break-in?"

"No, not exactly. Well, yes." She sighed. "Deputy, I don't know what I'm looking for, but the state police haven't been very forthcoming with information on the MacBriarty murder. I thought that since that knife was dropped in the same building where Mac was stabbed a few weeks later, maybe . . . Well, I guess I'm just fishing. I shouldn't have bothered you."

"Well . . . we do have pictures of the knife. Would that help?"

She caught her breath. "Of course you do! Thank you. That would help a lot. At least, it would give me something to putter around at. Is it all right if I come get the photos tomorrow?"

9

Nate hurried up Felicia's walkway, shivering despite his thick jacket, knit cap, and warm gloves. He hoped this cold snap wouldn't last long.

Emily opened the door and launched herself into his arms. "I'm so glad you're back."

He chuckled and maneuvered her inside so he could shut the door then returned her embrace. "What have you been up to?"

"Forensics."

"Oh yeah?"

"Yeah." She took his coat and hung it in the closet.

"Hello, Nate," Felicia called from the kitchen. "Do you want some coffee?"

"Sounds good, thanks." Nate let Emily lead him to the sofa. Her laptop was set up on the coffee table.

"I've been researching that knife," she said.

"What knife?"

"The one the burglar dropped at Jeff's when we were there."

"Oh, the pocketknife?" She placed two eight-by-ten photographs in his hands. He looked at them then turned them over and read the labels on the backs. "Where did you get these?"

"From Deputy Young. He told me Blakeney came and got the knife from them last month."

"No kidding?" Nate pondered what that might mean. "So what are you doing about it?"

She wrinkled up her face in distaste. "Well, I've been busy, but it hasn't told me a lot." She sat on the sofa, and Nate seated himself beside her.

"Tell me what you've got."

"It's a very common brand of knife. They sell it lots of places. They have several inexpensive models."

Nate nodded.

She moved the mouse, and the screen on her laptop cleared. "Look at this. It's the manufacturer's Web site."

Nate peered at the images on the screen. "Oh yeah, I've seen a lot of those."

"Of course you have. You sell them in the marina store."

He flicked a glance at her then back at the screen. "You sure?"

"Yes. Not the exact same model that the burglar dropped, but the same brand. I went over to the marina this morning and looked over the ones in stock. Then I talked to your mother, and she looked up her inventory records. The Baxter Marina has carried this brand for fifteen years, but you never actually stocked this model."

"Well, that's kind of a relief."

She nodded. "That would be too creepy if the thief bought his knife at your store. It's not one of the models they show on the Web site now. Your mom figures it's probably a few years old."

"So . . . where does that get us?"

She frowned and raised her hands in futility. "Nowhere, really. Anyone could have owned it. They could have bought it just about anywhere a few years back. And we don't know that it has anything to do with Mac. Probably not. I mean, obviously he wasn't stabbed with this knife."

"No, it was in the county sheriff's evidence locker when Mac was killed."

"Right. And the autopsy showed that the knife that killed him was bigger, anyway. Maybe a hunting knife." She leaned back and crossed her arms across her chest. "I

128

called Blakeney and told him everything I'd found out."

"What did he say?"

"To stay out of it."

Nate eyed her keenly. She sounded slightly put out but not angry or weepy. "You okay?"

"Yes. He did tell me one largish item that I can use in the paper this week, which is a relief, because we really need to give the readers something fresh on this case."

"What was that?"

"He said the medical examiner has confirmed that none of Jeff's knives they confiscated was the murder weapon."

"Hey, that's great. Does Jeff know?"

"I don't know. If not, he'll know when he reads the *Journal.* But I hope the police tell him first." Emily shrugged. "Of course, that doesn't let Jeff off. As Blakeney so delicately put it, there could be other weapons Mr. Lewis owned of which we know not the current location."

Felicia came in carrying a tray with three mugs, a sugar bowl, and a quart of milk.

"Here we go, folks."

"Thanks, Felicia." Nate accepted a mug of coffee and set it on a coaster beside the laptop. "Well, Em, it sounds as though your research about the knife wasn't totally wasted. It gave you and Blakeney some common ground to discuss, if nothing else."

He could tell by her expression that Emily wasn't satisfied. She pursed her lips and reached for the sugar bowl.

"Whatever."

"Come on, babe, don't pout," he said.

"Who's pouting?"

"Not me," Felicia said. "The basketball team at Aswontee is playing tonight. The winner goes to the tournament. We're all going, right?"

Nate looked eagerly at Emily. "Oh yeah. What do you say, Em? Aswontee Eagles, all the way!"

Her frowned morphed painfully into a smile. "Okay. This could be the game of the year."

"I'm writing the story," Felicia said, "but you can take the pictures."

Emily reached out and closed the laptop.

Two weeks later, Nate seated Emily at a table with his mother and Dad Phillips at a fancier restaurant than he usually patronized. He felt conspicuous in his uniform, with the new badge gleaming on his chest. The grueling course at the Maine Criminal Justice Academy was over, and he was now a sworn officer of the Penobscot County Sheriff's Department.

"So, seafood all around?" Jared asked as Nate sat down.

"I want scallops," said Nate's mother. "They never get deep-sea scallops at the Lumberjack, and I've been hankering for some."

"I think I'll try the fish chowder," Emily said, perusing the menu.

"That's not enough," the pastor chided. "What else?"

"A salad."

He shook his head. "Well, I'm with Connie. Scallops for me. Nate?"

"I'll take the fish and chips. And don't worry about Emily." Nate grinned at her. "She'll outdo us all when it comes to dessert."

Nate's stepfather had insisted on the celebratory meal in Waterville before they headed northward for Baxter and home. Now that the graduation ceremony was over, Nate realized how hungry he was and appreciated Jared's thoughtfulness.

"I'm so proud of you!" His mother leaned over to kiss him on the cheek.

"Aw, Mom, people are watching." Nate grimaced, but he wasn't really upset.

Emily just smiled, but when the waitress came and his parents were giving their orders, she bent toward him and whispered,

131

"I'm proud of you, too."

Could his life get any better?

"So, Nate, you'll be working mostly in northern Penobscot County?" the pastor asked.

"That's right. It lets me keep living in Baxter, which is a plus. Emily and I didn't want to have to move away."

Emily nodded. "It should work out very well for us."

"Have you two thought about where you'll live after you get married this summer?" his mother asked.

"We'll probably stay at Emily's cottage on the island as long as we can. When it gets too cold . . . well, we haven't really talked about it, but I'm sure we will." He glanced at Emily, but she was no help. Her cheeks flushed, and she looked away. Nate could see that this was a definite oversight on his part. "I mentioned once living at the marina, but the conversation was interrupted. I guess I assumed we'd live there during the winter."

"That's fine, if you want to," his mother said, "but Jonathan and Allison Woods came by the other day and asked me if we still planned to sell the business, and if the house goes with it."

That caught Nate by surprise. "I knew

they were interested in buying the marina, but they told us last fall they didn't have the money. And Jon's got the garage. I figured they'd keep that."

"Well, Allison's father died, and they've come into some money." His mother sipped her water. "Now Jon's thinking he'd like to sell the garage and their house and buy the marina and our house, if you want to sell."

"It's not up to me, Mom," Nate told her. "You own it."

"Now, honey, you've worked as hard as your father and I ever did, and since he died you've kept the place going. It's always been your home, and since your father passed away, I've considered the property and the business to be half yours."

"Thanks, that's very generous. But you know I haven't done anything at the marina since October. Allison has kept the store running all winter, and I've got to admit I like the freedom I've had, not being tied down all the time. Now that you've given up the post office and they moved it downtown, I guess I thought we'd just sell the business and maybe keep the house."

His mother reached over and squeezed his hand. "If you don't want to sell the house, we don't have to. But you're right. You're not working at the marina anymore, and Allison is doing a pretty good job of running it. If Jon sells the garage and they both work at it, I'm sure they can do as well as your father and I did. If you kids want to live at the marina house, we can probably work something out with them."

A renewed sense of loss hit Nate as he thought about the old days, with Dad handling the boat rentals while Mom manned the post office, and both of them working in the store. A lump rose in his throat. He'd grown up a part of it. Things wouldn't be the same without the marina. He swallowed hard and pressed his lips together, trying to find the appropriate response. "Thank you, Mom. Let me think about it, and we'll talk later, okay?"

"Sure."

"Perhaps you and Emily would like to discuss this in private, after you've had time to think it over," the pastor said softly.

Emily looked up at Nate with wide eyes. "Whatever you want to do is fine with me."

The pastor smiled. "Well, Nate, it sounds like you and Emily ought to decide where you want to live, and then you and Connie can work out what you both want to do."

An hour later they left the restaurant and went out into the cold, mid-March evening. With a light snow falling, the Maine winter refused to give up its hold.

Connie looked up at the swirling flakes. "I was hoping we were done with this for another year."

Dad Phillips chuckled. "Impatient, aren't you, my dear? We always get snow into April."

"Yeah," Nate agreed. "It's not even officially spring until tomorrow, Mom." His cell phone rang as they walked toward the pastor's car, and he pulled it from his pocket and answered it before getting into the backseat beside Emily.

"Hey, Nate! It's Jeff. I'm almost ready to reopen the lodge. Can you and Emily come next weekend, before the guests start coming?"

"That sounds like fun."

"Everything's redone. You've gotta see it."

Nate smiled and climbed into the car. "I'll ask Emily. I'm not sure if she has anything planned for the weekend."

"What?" she whispered.

After Nate finished the conversation, he relayed the gist of it to her. "Jeff has invited us to spend a couple of nights at the lodge. The remodeling's done, and he wants to show it off. He's reserved two guest rooms for us, and he's also invited his brother and sister and their families."

"Fun!" Emily cried. "I'm glad he feels like celebrating."

"Yeah. And getting his brother and sister up here is a real accomplishment, from what he's told me. I don't think they get together more than a few times a year."

"Will the lodge be taking guests in time for opening day?" Connie asked.

"Yes, he says he'll be open April first, right on time." The first day of fishing season was always a big day in the town of Baxter. It marked the return of sportsmen to Blue Heron Lake and the opening of most of the town's seasonal businesses. Fishermen flocked to the area, searching for open water to cast their lines in. Although the ice wouldn't be completely out on the huge lake for a few more weeks, Jeff's guides could usually find running streams where the ice had given way. By early May all the ice would have thawed from the lake, and the real tourist season would begin.

"Jeff told me Sunday that all the staff is coming back this week," the pastor said, pulling out of the parking lot. "He sounded very excited about getting things back to normal over there."

"Yeah, he's been pretty glum since Mac was killed," Nate agreed. "I wish Blakeney had found some evidence pointing to the killer."

"At least he didn't arrest Jeff," Emily said. "Yet."

Emily slipped her hand into his. "Eventually this thing will be cleared up, I'm sure."

"It's been almost three months," Connie noted. "I'm glad the renovations went ahead as planned."

"Yeah, things like that usually take longer than you expect," Nate said.

"And cost more," the pastor added.

Nate leaned over and kissed Emily. She squeezed his hand then sat back primly. He sighed and sat back in contentment. Life with Emily, whether in the tiny cottage on Grand Cat Island or at the rambling marina house where he'd grown up or some other place as yet undisclosed, would be fantastic.

Jeff's brother, Ian, and sister, Phoebe, had already arrived when Emily and Nate entered the lodge Friday evening. Try as she might, Emily couldn't remember either of them from her childhood days in Baxter. She remembered Jeff, who was a year ahead of her and Nate in school and rode the bus with them to the high school in Aswontee until he graduated. But Ian and Phoebe were several years older than Jeff, and she'd had little interaction with them that she could recall.

Phoebe and her husband, Kent Forster, had brought their twelve-year-old son, Derek, while Ian mentioned that it was his weekend to have "the kids" — Will, age fourteen, and Chelsea, eleven. The three young cousins were full of energy, and they sparked flippant remarks off each other.

The adults were sipping coffee with Jeff in his private quarters, and the youngsters, after brief introductions to Nate and Emily, dashed outside to do some moonlight snowboarding on the slope behind the lodge.

Phoebe had the same thick, dark hair as Jeff. She studied Emily with keen green eyes. She wore stretch ski pants and a red cable-knit sweater. Emily hoped the ivory sweater her mother had made her for Christmas held up under Phoebe's obvious scrutiny. She figured she couldn't go wrong with her black slacks, though they weren't quite as sophisticated as Phoebe's outfit.

Kent greeted them then sank back onto the sofa beside his wife with his mug of coffee cradled in his hands. Ian, by contrast, seemed eager to talk. Emily could see a slight resemblance between him and his younger brother, Jeff, but Ian's coloring was lighter, and his eyes were more hazel than green. Ian bared his life to them in less than five minutes — his years of building up his insurance business and his rancorous breakup with Natalie after ten years of marriage. Phoebe listened with a pained smile and interrupted with a description of the small but thriving health food store she and Kent owned in Bangor. Emily's impression was unmistakable. If she hadn't been there, Phoebe would have told her older brother to shut up.

"Nate, Emily, let me take you up to your rooms," Jeff said after a few minutes of small talk. "I want to see your reaction to the transformation."

"He's really done a terrific job," Phoebe said. "It looks like a different place."

Jeff grinned. "Thanks. It was a big job, but I think our clients will appreciate it." He led them up the stairs, carrying Emily's suitcase. Nate followed, bringing his own luggage.

Emily realized at once that Jeff was taking her to the same room she'd had at Thanksgiving.

"I hope you didn't get rid of the pine bedroom set," she said as he paused before the door.

"Oh, no. I kept the furnishings. Couldn't afford to replace them."

She nodded. "Great. It's good stuff, and very comfortable."

Jeff swung the door open and stood back. She and Nate entered, and Emily inhaled deeply.

"Oh, this is fantastic, Jeff!"

The warm, natural woodwork still gave her a nostalgic feeling, but two interior walls were now papered in a lilac floral design. The comforter and pillow shams echoed the purple, green, and white tones of the room. To her left was a door that had not been there before.

She glanced at Jeff then stepped forward to examine the bathroom.

"Wow!" The new white fixtures had a Victorian flavor, with a pedestal sink and gold-toned faucets. The toilet and glassed-in shower left no doubt the plumbing was state-of-the-art, but the gold-framed mirror and embroidered sampler on the wall added to the old-fashioned charm.

"You like it?" Jeff asked, unable to suppress his proud grin.

"It's a dream," Emily said.

"Lisa Cookson helped me pick out the linens and decorations."

Emily smiled at the timid pride on his face. Lisa, the desk clerk, must be special to Jeff. "And you put in ten new bathrooms?"

"Yup. I lost four guest rooms overall to get the space, but I had to do it. It'll take a while for the investment to pay off, but we're booked solid into July already, so I'm not afraid of losing money this year."

They went across the hall to Nate's room next and admired the new decor. Bedroom and bath had been done over in a beige and blue color scheme, and Nate nodded with approval.

"Plenty of outlets. I can shave in the morning."

Jeff laughed. "You guys have no idea how relieved I am to finally have all the work done."

"I'll bet," Nate said.

"No, really," Jeff went on. "The plumber broke his ankle skiing in January, which delayed things a couple of weeks until he located someone to take over for him, and the electrician dragged his feet until I had to threaten to hire someone else if he didn't finish on time."

"That's really rough." Nate shook his head.

"Well, everything looks great now," Emily assured Jeff. She looked out the window and took in the view of the forest. The ground between it and the lodge was still blanketed in ten inches of snow. "You've still got the ambiance, but something tells me your guests will be a lot cozier now."

"Thanks," Jeff said. "You know, I was a little nervous asking Phoebe and Ian and their families to come. I wasn't sure they would. But I guess they're all curious about the murder."

"Nobody mentioned it while we were together just now," Nate said.

"They asked me about it before you came." Jeff grimaced. "I gave them the short version. Phoebe is still prickly from a disagreement we had a year or two ago, but Ian wanted to know every gory detail. I told him I'd rather not go into it that deeply in front of the kids."

"They seem like nice kids," Emily told him.

"Oh yeah. They are, mostly. Typical modern kids, I guess. Anyway, I was glad you two showed up when you did."

"Well, thanks for having us. It will be fun to have enough people to get some games going around the fireplace."

Jeff smiled. "I'm hoping everyone will have a good time. I'd better go down and see if the kitchen crew is on schedule. You two can get settled. We're planning to have dinner at seven."

As he left them, Emily wondered if the

staff quarters on the third floor had been remodeled, too, and if anyone was now staying in Mac MacBriarty's old room. Some of the young women on duty must be staying overnight. Maybe she would have a chance to talk to Lisa later.

At the dinner table, Ian wasted no time in bringing up the subject of the lost money legend over their feast of roast beef, baked potatoes, green beans, and squash.

"So, Jeff, with all this remodeling, did you find any clues to the lumber baron's lost treasure?"

Phoebe laughed. "Honestly, Ian. You don't still believe that old taradiddle, do you?"

"You don't think there really was a treasure?" Jeff asked her.

Phoebe shrugged and reached for the salt. "If it's true — which I doubt — then I'm sure one of the lumberjacks found the old man's money and quietly made off with it."

Ian grinned at her across the table. "I hope not. I hope Jeff finds it now. I could use some extra cash."

"Oh yeah, Dad," said Will. "I really need a cell phone."

Ian scowled at him. "We talked about that already."

"Yeah, but if you got part of some old lumberjack's treasure . . ."

"Dream on," said Phoebe.

"No, get a job," Ian shot back at his son.

Emily glanced at Nate and cleared her throat. "Actually, I spoke to an attorney about this very topic a few months ago. I hate to disappoint anyone," — she smiled at Will and the other youngsters — "but the lawyer says that if by some miracle Mr. Eberhardt's treasure were found now on this property, it would belong to the current owner."

"Which would be Jeff," Ian said, the frown lines on his forehead deepening.

"Hey, Uncle Jeff," Will said with a sugary sweet smile, "I'm your favorite nephew, right?"

"Watch it," said Derek. "Who filled the wood boxes in the library and Uncle Jeff's study, hmm?"

"Boys," Chelsea muttered, rolling her eyes.

Phoebe gazed at Emily. "This attorney . . . someone acting for Jeff?"

"Oh no," Emily said. "I did a story about the lodge —"

"I saw it on the Web site," Ian said. "Well done."

"Oh, thank you." Emily smiled at Phoebe. "When I talked to Jeff about the treasure, he mentioned the possibility that the money is still out there, hidden somewhere, and how your grandfather left his will. I didn't think Maine law would allow anyone to bequeath a hypothetical asset like that, so I mentioned it to a lawyer I know slightly, without giving him any names."

"What did he say?" Kent asked.

Emily looked down the table at him in surprise. Phoebe's husband had seemed absorbed in his meal, and she hadn't thought he was listening to a word that was said. She decided not to tell them she had obtained a copy of their grandfather's will. That might seem overly nosy. She had a feeling Phoebe and Kent, and possibly Ian, too, would not understand her burning desire to investigate every mystery she encountered.

"Well, he said that if a person like your grandfather left something to 'all his living descendants,' it would be divided equally. But he left the property in Baxter — that is, this property, the lodge and its grounds, to your father."

Ian nodded. "Dad had two sisters. They got the family's house in Brewer. I think they sold it and divided the money, but Dad kept this property and developed the business."

"Right," Emily said. "What the lawyer explained to me was that your aunts, if they

145

are still living, and their children and grand-children, would have no claim to the treasure if it were found today. But neither would you and your sister, or your children."

"It all goes to Jeff?" Phoebe's eyebrows rose to meet her bangs.

"No fair!" Chelsea cried.

"Yes, because your father left the property to Jeff," Emily said.

Jeff shook his head. "Actually, I bought half interest from him a few years ago, and when he died, the three of us split the other half. I bought Ian's and Phoebe's shares from them before the estate was settled."

"Even more reason for you to be sole owner of the treasure if it's ever found on this land." Emily shrugged with a smile. "But after all, unless something changes, it's just a legend." She looked at Phoebe. "You're not really out anything because of your granddad's unenforceable will."

"Bummer," Will said and pushed back his chair. "May I be excused, Uncle Jeff?"

"Sure," Jeff replied. He'd been quiet during the discussion of Elisha Lewis's will, and Emily hoped she hadn't embarrassed or upset him.

"Me, too," said Derek, rising.

"What are you kids going to do?" Ian asked.

"Look for the treasure," Derek replied.

Phoebe laughed. "This place basically got torn apart from the inside over the last four or five months. You think you're going to find something nobody else has found?"

Derek frowned. "Well, maybe."

Chelsea laid down her napkin and stood up. "Come on, Derek. I'll help you make a list of places we can look tomorrow. It could be hidden somewhere outside."

"That's a good idea," Ian said. "Maybe it's in the old boathouse. I wonder how old that building is."

"Or the cabin out in the woods where the hunters stay sometimes," Will added.

"Why bother?" Phoebe leaned back in her chair. "If you find it, you'll only enrich Uncle Jeff."

Ian looked across the table at Emily, and his brow furrowed once more. "So Jeff would get it all."

The uneasy mood that had descended on them made Emily wish she had said nothing. She looked at Nate, attempting to telegraph her regret to him with her eyes. He fumbled for her hand under the edge of the table and gave it a squeeze.

Still, Nate's support wasn't enough to take away Emily's troubled thoughts.

A few hours later, Emily lay sleepless in

her room, thinking about the turmoil that seemed to simmer just below the surface among the Lewis siblings. She'd grown up an only child, always wishing she'd had sisters and brothers. Seeing this tension made her wonder if she hadn't romanticized the bliss of large families. She rolled over with a sigh. When she couldn't sleep, her habit was to pray, and she started a petition in her mind.

Lord, thank You for giving Nate and me this weekend with Jeff and his family. Help them to get along, and help me to be more careful about —

A loud thumping on the wall opposite her pretty bathroom jerked her out of her drowsiness, and she sat up in the dark, her heart racing.

10

Emily slid out from under her covers and placed her feet on the floor. Remembering the break-in at the lodge in the fall, and Mac's death, she wondered briefly if she should wake Nate or Jeff before investigating the noise. Nate's room was on the opposite side of the hall, and she was fairly sure Jeff had said there wasn't anyone staying in the room next to hers.

She stood up, pulled her bathrobe on over her pajamas, and took a flashlight from the nightstand. All sorts of thoughts flooded her mind. Another intruder? The murderer returning to retrieve something?

She breathed deeply. "It's your imagination," she told herself firmly. "Or it's one of the kids poking around." The murderer had escaped undetected the week after Christmas. He wouldn't come back after all this time. Still, she moved carefully and quietly to the door, turned the knob slowly, and stepped into the hallway.

A dim light shone from beneath the door of the room next to her own. She tiptoed closer and put an ear to the door. Someone was definitely moving around in there. Maybe someone was occupying the room after all and she'd been mistaken. Unsure of what to do, she raised her hand and tapped softly on the fresh cream-colored paint of the door panel. The light went out, and the sounds from within stopped. She wondered if the person inside had heard her and turned out the light hoping to avoid discovery.

Maybe not. Maybe the occupant had gotten into bed and shut the light off without hearing her timid knock. She held perfectly still and waited, but there was no more sound from behind the door, and the light did not go back on.

She hesitated another minute, but at last she decided to return to bed. More likely than not, one of Jeff's relatives had changed rooms without her knowledge. She didn't want to rouse the house for nothing.

She slept lightly, waking a few more times in the night, but no more noises came from the room next door. It occurred to her that one of the youngsters might have decided to do a little treasure hunting or exploring.

When she awoke Saturday morning, sunlight brightened her room, and she knew she had at last had a few solid hours of sleep. She smelled the aroma of hot coffee and glanced at her bedside clock. It was nearly eight o'clock. She dressed quickly, brushed her hair and washed her face, and headed down the stairs to find Jeff and Nate.

"Well, sleepyhead," Nate said, grinning at her as she entered the dining room. "Finally decided to join us?"

Everyone else was already up and halfway through their breakfast.

"I didn't sleep very well," said Emily. "I kept waking up." She watched everyone at the table as she spoke, hoping to catch some trace of reaction. Perhaps someone had been poking around last night where they didn't belong. But everyone seemed engrossed in the meal.

"Sorry to hear that. There's still plenty of food," said Jeff. "Help yourself. Pancakes, scrambled eggs, sausages."

"It looks wonderful." Emily slid into the chair Nate pushed out for her.

"Orange juice?" Nate asked.

"Thanks."

As he filled her glass, he asked, "So, why couldn't you sleep? Still fretting over the guest list for the wedding?"

"I heard something," Emily whispered to him.

"Heard what?" His voice was equally low.

"Can't talk now. But Jeff needs to hear this, too."

After breakfast, Nate collared Jeff and told him Emily wanted to speak to them privately. The three of them converged in Jeff's private office while the others were suiting up to go out snowmobiling.

"What's the trouble, Em?" Jeff asked.

Emily sat on the loveseat and pushed her honey blond hair away from her face. "I heard noises last night, Jeff. I thought you said the room next to mine was vacant."

"Well, it is." Jeff frowned.

She arched her eyebrows. "I'm positive I heard someone moving around in there last night around eleven o'clock."

"The room's ready for guests arriving Friday," said Jeff. "But no one should have been in there last night. Are you sure you heard something?"

Emily's eyes shone and her face turned pink. Nate could tell she was a little annoyed.

"I'm positive. I even got out of bed and stepped into the hall. Light was coming from underneath the door. I thought maybe you'd switched someone's room last night and I didn't know it."

Nate felt his heartbeat accelerate. "Jeff, maybe we should have a look." With memories of the intruder incident and the murder still fresh on his mind, he didn't want to let this go without investigating, especially if there was any question of Emily's safety.

"You're right," said Jeff. "We'll check the room. But I appreciate your telling me in private. I don't want everyone else speculating and making up stories. Let's keep this quiet."

"No problem," said Nate. "My lips are sealed. Come on, Em."

The three of them went upstairs, where Emily paused outside her room. "I heard the sounds coming from beyond my bedroom wall, on the side opposite my bathroom," she explained. "So it had to have been the bedroom next to mine."

Jeff nodded. "The bath for that guest room is on the other side. The shape of the room is a mirror image of yours." He approached the door next to Emily's and tried the knob. The door swung open. "That's odd," he said. "Let's take a look."

The double bed was made up with a red, white, and blue quilt. Extra blankets were stacked neatly on top of a trunk in the corner, and everything was tidy and clean.

Jeff surveyed the room. "Nothing's out of place. Are you sure you didn't mistake the room number?"

"I'm positive. Like I said, I'd gone to bed, and I heard a noise. Someone walking around and a thumping — almost like someone knocking. It sounded like it was just on the other side of the wall."

Nate thought she sounded a bit defensive. He took her hand. "Jeff, do you think someone was sneaking around? One of the kids, maybe?" He didn't like the idea that more prowlers were breaking into the lodge, but he wanted to stand up for Emily even if it seemed an unlikely coincidence.

"There couldn't have been anyone in here. I keep the guest rooms locked."

Emily gave him a pointed look. "It wasn't locked just now."

"True. And that is odd. Our security isn't as tight as a hotel's would be, but we do keep the rooms locked so that one guest can't wander into another's room. My dad learned the hard way to do that. He had some pilfering about ten years ago. That's when we started this policy."

"So, no one had this room last night," Nate mused, opening the closet and taking a quick look inside.

"Right. No one was booked for this room until Friday. I wanted to give everyone as much privacy as possible, so I assigned the rooms with vacancies between the ones you and my family were occupying. And if someone came in from outside, I would have noticed a stranger in my own place."

Was he assuring them or trying to reassure himself, Nate wondered. "There's the staff. And you know someone got in before."

"I know. I'll talk to the maids. It's possible one of them made the room up and forgot to lock it."

"But they wouldn't have been working at 11:00 p.m.," Emily insisted.

"No, they wouldn't. In fact, none of them stayed here overnight last night. They were all gone by nine o'clock."

Emily gave them a rueful smile. "This is the part where Lord Peter Wimsey would dust for fingerprints. I hate that we can't do anything without police approval. And they aren't going to want to come out here and investigate a non crime."

"Can you do anything, Nate?" Jeff asked.

"I don't have a fingerprint kit."

"So, do you think I should report this?"

Nate shrugged his shoulders. "There's nothing definite. Talk to the staff. One of them might have an explanation."

"Yeah," said Emily. "I don't think you should call the police. If they sent someone out here, it would probably be Detective Blakeney, and you know he doesn't like me, anyway."

"I'm not on his list of favorite people, either." Jeff's face squeezed into a grimace, and Emily wished she hadn't mentioned the detective.

As they went down the stairs to the lobby, Ian came in from the side porch.

"Hey, Nate! Sam Pottle is taking us over to Black Mountain, and we've got an extra snowmobile. Do you want to go? Phoebe decided not to go with us when she heard we'd be out all morning. You could both come."

Nate looked to Emily for a clue as to her feelings. "How about it, Em? Want to go?"

She smiled a bit apologetically. "You go ahead. I brought my laptop. If it's all the same to you, I'll get some work done on my story about Raven Miller's new business. I promised Felicia I'd write it up over the weekend."

Nate hesitated. He did like riding a snowmobile, and he hadn't had a chance all winter. He knew Emily would barely notice he was gone if she got immersed in writing her article about the Christian camping center on the island.

"You sure?"

"Yes, but you go ahead. You'll have fun with Kent and Ian and the kids."

"Okay."

"Yeah!" Ian said. "There's no rule that says the lovebirds have to spend every minute together, huh?"

Jeff eyed him sternly. "Just stay away from the lake, Ian. I know you've got Sam with you, but the ice is getting soft. Make sure you warn the kids."

"Oh, relax, little brother." Ian scowled at him. "I grew up in this territory, too, remember? I know better than to take a sled out on the lake this late in the season."

"Right. Sorry. Have fun." Jeff's smile faded as he turned toward the kitchen.

Nate hurried to put on his cold-weather gear. When he was ready, he found Emily setting up her laptop at one of the tables in the empty dining room. He clomped in wearing his awkward snowmobile boots and suit.

"I'll see you later, babe."

She grinned at him. "You look like you're ready for an arctic expedition. Have a great time."

He stooped to kiss her then whispered in her ear, "These guys wouldn't be my first picks for a serious expedition, but we'll have fun."

Sam Pottle, one of the certified Maine guides Jeff employed for hunting, fishing, and snowmobiling parties, led them over a network of trails through second-growth forest. Although the snow cover had compacted and would be gone in a few weeks, there was plenty of white stuff for their outing.

They broke into the open a mile from the lodge and skirted a snow-covered hay field, staying with the marked trail. On the far side, they headed up an incline. The trail wound about through brush for a short way then brought them out on a woods road. An hour later they came to a halt on the high, rounded hill known locally as Black Mountain.

Sam shut off his engine, and Nate, Ian, Kent, and Will did the same. Chelsea climbed off the back of Ian's snowmobile. Derek had ridden with Kent. They all got off and walked a few yards to the highest point of the summit.

"Wow! What a view of the lake!" Chelsea squealed.

"Is that the lodge?" Derek asked, pointing downward to the lakeside building. Gray smoke issued steadily from its central chimney.

"It sure is," said Ian.

Will scooped up some sticky snow and formed a snowball with his mittened hands. "Hey, Chelsea!"

When his sister looked his way, he tossed it at her. It splattered on the front of her zippered snowmobile suit.

"You asked for it!" Chelsea dove for a handful of snow.

"Uh-oh!" Derek scurried for cover and found a spot behind a boulder. Chelsea and Will found niches of their own and started making snowballs.

"Something tells me we're in the line of fire," Kent said.

Nate laughed and moved a few feet away from the potential battlefield. "This is great. I haven't had time to get out and do something like this for months."

Ian shrugged. "Well, it seemed like a big deal to Jeff that we come for a visit, though why he should care, I don't know."

"He's worked hard," Kent said. "All those renovations to the lodge. He wanted you all to see it before the paint gets scratched up."

"Yeah, well." Ian scowled. "Don't you get the feeling sometimes that he's rubbing our noses in it?"

"What do you mean?" Nate asked, looking from Ian to Kent. Sam had strolled off and was getting something out of the storage compartment on his snowmobile.

"I just mean that he's done all right with the lodge the past few years."

"Isn't that the idea?" Nate eyed him carefully.

Kent gave him a thin smile. "I know what he means. Phoebe's a little touchy about it, too. They both agreed to sell out to Jeff at the time, but Phoebe wonders now if maybe they got the raw end of the deal. Is that what you're saying, Ian?"

"Well, Jeff seems to have plenty of money. He must have put a fortune into this remodeling."

Kent shrugged. "He might have taken a loan. And when he bought you guys out, we put the money we got for Phoebe's share into the store. We wouldn't have it now if she'd kept her part of Lakeview Lodge."

"Yeah, but . . ." Ian shook his head. "The lodge was kind of run down then, and it seemed like it wasn't making much profit. I didn't see much point in hanging on to it. Personally, I wanted to get out of Baxter and do something different."

"I think you said you have your own business now, don't you?" Nate asked.

"Yeah. Insurance. But that's not the point."

"What is the point?" Kent seemed to be pushing Ian. Nate began to wish they hadn't stopped to chat.

"My point is that Jeff's done all right for himself. It rankles me to think he would get the whole of old Eberhardt's treasure if we found it."

Kent laughed. "Whoever said life is fair? You knew about your grandfather's will when you agreed to sell to Jeff."

"Yeah, and so did Phoebe. But because of the will, we thought we'd get a share of the treasure if anyone found it."

"Oh, come on." Kent shook his head and laughed. "You guys must have hunted for that stupid treasure when you were kids. Phoebe told me she used to dig around the yard, hoping to find it was buried there."

"Yeah, we did. But we didn't actually live here. We used to spend most of the summer at the lodge. But when we were here, we had to work. Jeff and I did do some looking, though. We climbed over every inch of the equipment shed, and then Dad told us it wasn't even there when Eberhardt died."

Kent smiled. "Well, it's a moot point, anyhow. There's no treasure."

Sam approached them carrying a Thermos

jug. "Anybody want some coffee?"

"That sounds great," said Nate.

"Dad! My feet are cold." Chelsea waddled over in her bulky snowsuit. Her face was flushed, and part of a smashed snowball ornamented her pink knit hat.

Sam handed the jug and several Styrofoam cups to Kent.

"Here, take your boots off and put your feet on this." He flipped up the engine cover on the nearest snowmobile.

Chelsea stared at him. "Really?"

"Sure." Sam felt the part of the engine he had pointed to with his gloved hand. "The engine's not hot enough to burn you now, but it's still warm enough to toast your tootsies."

Chelsea laughed and sat down to take her boots off. When she was sitting with her stocking feet balanced up in the air, her father picked her up and carried her to the snowmobile.

"Oof, you're getting heavy, kiddo," Ian said.

Chelsea hugged him and stuck her feet out to rest on top of the engine.

"Better?" Sam asked.

"Yes, thank you."

The boys came over, and Ian let Will have a cup of coffee.

"Me, too," said Derek.

"Nah, it'll stunt your growth," said Kent.

"Aw, Dad!"

Kent shrugged and put his half-empty cup in Derek's hands. "Don't tell your mother. She'll fuss about caffeine and I don't know what."

Nate smiled and swigged his coffee. The health food store must have been Phoebe's idea, not Kent's. At least they'd quit talking as if Jeff had taken advantage of them. He wondered if Ian resented his brother enough to poke around the lodge at night. Or to ride up here to Baxter other times and break in to look for the treasure.

11

"Hey, Emily, I thought you might be ready for some cocoa. I know I am." Jeff set a tray down across the table from her and smiled wearily.

"That looks great," she admitted. She clicked on her keyboard to save her article and glanced at the time in the corner of the screen. She'd been working most of the morning.

"How's it coming?" Jeff placed a steaming mug before each of them, along with a bag of marshmallows and two spoons. He set the tray on the vacant table behind him.

"Good. I just finished my rough draft. Now I only need to edit a little and write cutlines for the pictures."

"Did you say the story is about Raven Miller?" He opened the marshmallows and offered her the bag.

"Yes, this story is about her new family camping center."

"Seems like I heard she was making big changes on the island."

Emily plopped two marshmallows into her cocoa, picked up her spoon, and dunked them. "She's given up the Vital Women retreats. She told me she has no appetite for all that New Age stuff anymore. It's amazing, the way she's changed since last summer."

"And she's turning her property into a family campground."

"Sort of. It will be a Christian retreat center. Church groups and families are booking vacations, and she plans to have a different speaker each week. You should talk to Raven. Maybe some of your guests will want to take a boat out to Grand Cat this summer and go to some of the meetings." Emily sipped her cocoa and licked the sticky melted marshmallow off her lips. "She'll still have recreational activities like she always has — swimming, snorkeling, hiking, kayaking. And Pastor Phillips has helped her line up some terrific speakers. You could probably work out a deal with her if your guests wanted to go over for a barbecue before the evening meetings."

"Is your story going to be in Tuesday's paper?"

"Yeah," Emily said.

"I'll clip it and get a schedule from Raven. Do you have her address?"

"Yes, she's got a year-round place in Orono. But she'll be in town getting the retreat center ready as soon as the ice is out."

Jeff leaned back in his chair. "Must be frustrating for you island dwellers not to be able to get to your homes in the spring and fall."

Emily smiled. "Well, it's not for long, just that time when the ice isn't thick enough to hold you up. Truly Vigue took me out on a snowmobile a couple of times this winter so I could check the cottage."

"When do you plan to move out to the island again? Memorial Day?"

"No, I won't wait that long. I'm like Raven — as soon as a boat can get out there, I'm moving. Oh, I've enjoyed staying with Felicia this winter, but I like being on my own, and I miss the cottage."

"You'll freeze."

She shook her head. "I've got a fireplace, and Nate put a little woodstove in for me last fall."

Just then, Phoebe entered the dining room.

"Hi. Mmm, any more chocolate?"

Jeff stood with a chuckle. "Come on, I

166

think we can find you a cup. Lucille is taking her break, though."

They went through the door to the kitchen, and Emily reached for the bag of marshmallows. She floated two fresh ones on the surface of her cooling cocoa. She was glad Jeff had invited her and Nate for the weekend. As she reached for her spoon, the sunlight streaming through the window sparkled off her diamond ring, and she held it out to admire it anew. Lakeview Lodge would always hold happy memories for her.

"So, Phebes," Jeff said as he and his sister came back into the dining room, "I meant to ask you. Did you or Kent go into guest room 6 during the night?"

"Huh?" Phoebe stopped and stared at him. "What are you talking about? You think I kicked Kent out of our room or something?"

"That room is supposed to be vacant, but someone went in there last night."

"Oh, great! Are you accusing me of something?"

"No." Jeff held up one hand. "I'm just trying to figure out why someone went —"

"You think I'd go sneaking around at night? Treasure hunting, I suppose. You don't want the kids looking for the treasure, do you?"

"Was it the kids?" Jeff asked.

Phoebe's jaw dropped. "You twist everything I say. Just like always."

"Oh, come on, Phebes. Don't take it that way."

"I said I didn't go in there. What part of that don't you understand?" Phoebe whirled, nearly slopping her cocoa over the edge of the mug.

Jeff stood watching her as she stomped into the lobby and up the stairs. He sighed, and his posture wilted. After a moment, he turned and walked over to Emily's table.

"Sorry about that."

"It wasn't your fault," she said. "Phoebe's a tad sensitive, I'd say. Sit down and finish your cocoa."

"If I'd had any idea how touchy she was . . ."

"Marshmallows are an antidote to depression, you know." She held the bag up.

"Really?" He smiled, and Emily tossed him the bag.

"So, are you hosting the fishing derby again this year?" she asked.

"Yup. It's a tradition here at the lodge on Memorial Day weekend. Every room is booked."

"Terrific. I remember how much my Dad used to look forward to it. He won a new fishing rod one year."

"Yeah, the local fishermen love it. We get some of the same folks year after year. And now guys who came with their fathers twenty years ago are bringing their kids."

Emily flipped open her notebook and jotted herself a reminder note. "We'll be sure to give you some publicity. Get us the details as early as you can, and we'll do an advance."

"That'd be great. I asked Felicia to run the rules in the paper last year, but she said she didn't have space."

"Well, guess what. Now that we're doing two editions a week, we're usually begging for copy. I can pretty much guarantee you some good coverage. Photos, too."

"Sounds good. I was thinking of running an ad the week before and listing the prizes all the local businesses have donated." Jeff took a sip of his hot chocolate and set his cup down with a sigh. "I haven't had a chance to talk to you and Nate about this, but that cop, Blakeney, came out here again a couple of days ago."

"What did he want?"

"He said he was just touching base. More like keeping tabs on me." Jeff inhaled deeply. "I know he thinks I killed Mac. Every few weeks he comes around just to intimidate me."

"You're just the most convenient suspect. He has no evidence pointing to you." Emily watched him closely. Dark circles beneath Jeff's eyes and fine lines at the corners of his mouth made him look older than his twenty-seven years.

"I keep reminding myself of that. He has no proof because there is no proof. I would never kill anyone, let alone Mac. I liked him. We'd known each other for years. I had nothing against him."

"There was that incident over the moose hunt."

Jeff shook his head. "Blakeney tried to make something of that, but it was nothing. I'm not sure Mac really did it. If he did, he surely learned his lesson. I don't hold grudges. Why can't this thing just go away?"

Emily patted his sleeve. "I know it seems like this investigation is dragging on forever. It's been what? Two months since Mac died?"

"More like three. Don't you think they'd be able to do something? I mean, as long as they don't have another suspect, a lot of people probably think I did it."

"Oh, no. Don't say that. Come on, Jeff." Emily felt tears prickling in her eyes. "I didn't realize how badly this thing has been bothering you."

Jeff stuck a spoon in his mug and stirred his cocoa. "I'm sorry. I try not to think about it too much, and it doesn't seem to have hurt business. Most people from out of state don't know about the murder. A few Maine folks have mentioned it when they called for reservations. People who knew Mac, mostly. One couple even asked if they could stay in the room where the murder took place."

Emily winced. "That's a little gruesome. But you don't put guests up there, do you?"

"No, I told them the rooms in the staff quarters aren't available."

"Is anyone sleeping in there now?"

"No, not yet. The girls will be staying here this week to help get ready. And when we're running at our peak, I'll have to put someone in Mac's room. Probably one of the other guides. I don't think Royce or Sam would have any qualms about it. I had the room completely done over. Repainted, new mattress . . ." He shoved his chair back. "Well, hey. I've got guests arriving in a few days, and there's still a lot to do. Guess I'd better start acting like the boss and make sure we're ready. Thanks for listening, Emily."

"You're welcome. And you know we're

praying for you, don't you, Jeff?"

"Yeah. That helps. It reminds me that even if Detective Blakeney never solves this murder, God knows who did it."

The snowmobilers returned for a late lunch. The children recounted the tale of their journey with glittering eyes, but after they left the dining room, Phoebe lapsed into broody silence. The rest of the adults kept up a halfhearted conversation as they finished dessert. Emily wondered if Jeff was still smarting from the way his sister had turned on him, or if that was a common occurrence in the Lewis family.

Lisa came around with the coffeepot again, and Jeff smiled wearily up at her.

"Thanks, Lisa. I think I'll take this into my office. I need to make some calls. Excuse me, folks. Make yourselves at home this afternoon. Nate, we mentioned that I'd like to buy a couple of new canoes this spring. Maybe we can talk later."

"Sure," Nate said. When Jeff had exited, he leaned toward Emily. "I told Jeff he could just go over to the marina and pick out what he wants and tell Allison."

"Maybe he really wants to talk about something else," Emily said softly, not wanting to say much with Jeff's family present.

Phoebe refused coffee.

"Would you like some herbal tea, Mrs. Forster?" Lisa asked.

"No, thank you." Phoebe pushed back her chair and stood. She took a step away from the table then glared at her husband. "Kent?"

"Hmm?" He looked up at her while holding up his mug for Lisa to fill.

"I told you I want to pack. Don't drink that."

Kent sighed and set the mug down. "All right, if you say so." He smiled apologetically at Lisa as he rose. "Lunch was very good. Excuse me."

Phoebe's gaze landed on her older brother next. "Ian, I want to talk to you."

"So talk." Ian slurped his coffee and leaned back in his chair.

"In private."

"Phoebe," Kent said softly, but she only scowled at him.

"This is a family matter, Kent."

Kent winced and glanced at Emily and Nate. Emily managed a weak smile and slid her fork under her last bite of apple crumb pie. *I really shouldn't eat this, but who can resist Lucille's pies?* As soon as she got back to Felicia's, she'd have to implement a strict diet. Wedding dress mode.

"Ian?" Phoebe's voice rose to fingernails-on-chalk-board irritating.

"Yeah, yeah. I'm not done eating. I'll come upstairs in a bit."

Phoebe strutted out of the dining room with Kent following, his hands raised at shoulder height as though imploring, "Why me?"

Ian grinned at Nate and Emily. "My sister never got over not being queen."

"So, what are you all going to do this afternoon?" Nate asked, wearing an affable smile.

"Not sure. Will wants me to go out and do some snowboarding with the kids, but I'm getting kinda old for that. Maybe I'll tour the murder room. After Phoebe gets done complaining to me about whatever it is that's got her in such a snit. If she didn't want to come, she should have stayed home." He shook his head.

"It means a lot to Jeff that all of you are here," Emily said.

Ian drained his coffee cup then looked over at her. "I feel sorry for Kent sometimes."

About three o'clock that afternoon, while Nate waited for Emily to join him in the lobby, he was surprised to see the Forster

174

family coming down the stairs carrying their luggage. Ian and his children were close behind.

Jeff came from his office and walked between Kent and Phoebe. "Come on, Phebes, you don't want to leave now. We'll play some games tonight."

"No, I think we'd better get back to Bangor," Phoebe said. She sounded rather stiff, Nate thought.

"Kent?" Jeff turned to her husband.

"Hey, I'm just along for the ride," Kent said as they went out the door. "Nothing personal, Jeff. We'll see you again soon, I'm sure."

"Yeah, right," Will said bitterly.

Ian glared at him. "That's enough. Come on, Chelsea. Pull that lip in, or you'll trip over it." His glance swept over the room, and Nate jumped from his chair.

"Need some help?"

"No, we've got it."

Ian and the youngsters dragged their bags over the threshold, and Ian closed the front door. Nate let his pent-up breath out. Had angry words passed among the siblings this afternoon? He'd spent almost an hour with Jeff after lunch, looking over the fishing gear in the lodge's supply closet. Jeff hadn't mentioned the family tension, so Nate hadn't brought it up. Maybe Emily knew what that scene in the dining room meant, but he sure didn't. Well, Emily had agreed to meet him as soon as she was done with her article, so maybe he'd get the scoop from her.

Nate walked to the window and pushed the plaid curtain aside. Jeff stood helplessly in the parking lot, watching Ian and Kent load the bags.

"Hey, Will, Derek, Chelsea — you're coming for a visit this summer, right?" Jeff called.

"Sure, Uncle Jeff," Chelsea said.

"Yeah," Derek agreed.

Will looked doubtfully toward his father.

Jeff's shoulders slumped, but he stood his ground and waved until both vehicles were out of sight.

12

"Hey, what's up?"

Nate turned to see Emily coming down the stairway.

"Everybody's leaving."

Her eyes widened. "Really? I thought they were staying until tomorrow."

"Me, too, but Phoebe said they had to get home. I think she's upset with Jeff."

"Uh-oh."

Nate turned away from the window. "So, did you get your article all written?"

"Sure did," Emily said.

"How about we go snowshoeing, then?"

Her smile didn't convince him she was wild about the idea, even though the weather was mild.

"Where do you get so much energy?" she asked.

"I dunno. Just born that way, I guess. Come on, Em. This could be your last chance this year. The snow is going fast."

She sighed. "Okay, but if I fall down, you have to promise you won't laugh."

Jeff came in the front door and closed it firmly behind him. When he turned, his green eyes were troubled. "I'm sorry you guys were caught up in this mess. I never should have asked them to come."

"Oh, Jeff, don't feel bad." Emily went over and touched his sleeve. "I'm sorry Phoebe got angry with you."

He inhaled deeply. "She sent Kent down to my office a little while ago to break the news to me that they were all leaving early. Man, I thought Ian would be on my side. He and Phoebe fight like cats and dogs most of the time."

"He agrees with her on this . . . whatever it is?" Nate asked.

Jeff barked a short laugh. "Apparently."

Emily glanced at Nate then asked softly, "Is all this anger over the treasure, Jeff? I wish I hadn't said anything about your granddad's will last night."

Jeff ran a hand through his hair. "It may have started with that on the surface, but I think it's a lot deeper. It's money in general. I've made good on my inheritance. Phoebe and Kent have a store that's barely breaking even. Ian pretty much blew what he got and is paying the rest in child support. I think they believe that somehow I bilked them when I bought out their shares of the property."

Nate looked helplessly at Emily. He'd never had siblings, but perhaps being an only child wasn't such an awful thing. He couldn't imagine fighting over the marina.

"I'm really sorry, Jeff," he said. "Is there anything Emily and I can do?"

"Just stay and have a good time and . . . and add this miserable family to your prayer list, I guess."

"We will," Emily assured him. "We were talking about doing a little snowshoeing, but if there's something we can help you with . . ."

"No, go on. We've got a great weekend. Enjoy it while you can."

"Want to come with us?" Nate asked.

Jeff shook his head. "Thanks, but I'll stay here. I need to have the staff do up the rooms Ian and Phoebe used and log in some new reservations."

A short time later, Nate and Emily sat on the porch steps to buckle on the unwieldy footwear.

Nate loved the chance to get out into the pine woods. He'd always spent as much time outdoors as possible and had practically lived on the water in summer. He grinned over at Emily. "I'm glad you said yes."

"To this, or to marrying you?"

"Both. Well, I was thinking of this jaunt. You need to get out and get your blood moving more."

"Okay. Just don't expect me to be graceful as I move it. I'll probably keep stepping on the back end of these things. You know I'm not a great athlete."

Nate finished adjusting his straps, stood, and stamped each foot a couple of times to make sure the snowshoes were tight enough. "Need any help?"

"No, I think I'm ready." Emily pulled on her mittens.

He reached out a hand to help her stand.

"Where to?" she asked.

"Let's take the path along the lakeshore."

"Good. It's pretty flat. I don't think I'm up to doing hills on these things. I haven't been snowshoeing in at least eight years."

Nate set off at a good clip. When he reached the opening to the path, he looked back and found he'd outdistanced her by half the width of the parking lot.

"Sorry." He waited for her to catch up.

"Are you nervous or something?" she asked.

"About what?"

"Oh, I don't know. Let's see, what could be winding you up like this? There's the feuding Lewis family. Or maybe it's the fact that you're starting work Monday with the sheriff's department. That'll be your first official day on the job."

Nate squinted at her. "Well, I'm excited about it. I don't know as I'd say I'm nervous."

She nodded soberly. "That's good, I guess. I'm trying not to be."

"Aw, Em, you know there's nothing to worry about."

"You'll be telling criminals to quit doing what they're doing."

"That's one way to put it." He smiled. "Don't worry. You know God will be watching over me."

"Yeah."

Nate reached out and lifted her chin until she looked him in the eye. "I suppose I might be a little nervous about this house thing. Selling the marina house."

"Or not selling it. You told me that Jon and Allison have a lead on a rental in case you decide to keep the house. Honey, you can keep the house if you want to. Your mom said so, and I'm willing to live there with you after the wedding."

"But then Mom wouldn't get her share of

the income from it."

"Do you think she needs it?"

"Well . . . no, not if we sell the business. I suppose she'll be pretty well fixed. There's no mortgage or anything. But I hate to disappoint Jon and Allison."

"What's the rental they're looking at?"

"Bridget Kaplin at Blue Heron Realty showed it to them. It's a fairly new house on the Aswontee Road. It wouldn't be as convenient for them — it's about three miles from the marina. But they're happy to buy the business from us, with or without the house."

Emily stood on tiptoe and kissed his lips lightly. "There's no need to feel guilty if you want to keep that house. It's your home. But we can keep praying about it for a while if you're not comfortable with it. You don't want to make a decision you'll regret later."

"Thanks." He looked down into her blue eyes. "When I really stop and think about it and don't let my emotions get in the way — thinking about Dad and the past — then the house doesn't matter so much to me. I love law enforcement. I never want to run the marina again. I want to be a police officer. Maybe you and I should look at that rental house."

"But you love the marina house," she said.

"I can't imagine you living three miles from the water."

"I do love the lake. And we need a place to keep a boat so we can have access to the island."

"It sounds to me like you want to keep the house," Emily said. "Personally, I've always liked it, but I can be happy anyplace where we'll be warm and comfortable next winter."

Nate had a mental image of the two of them squeezing into Emily's current quarters. "There's one thing I know for sure: You may get along just fine living with Felicia, but there is no way I will ever rent a room at her house."

Emily laughed. "Got it. Now, Mr. Deputy, we've only got a couple of hours or so of daylight left by my calculations. Let's get this hike on the road . . . I mean, the trail."

Nate laughed and set off at a moderate pace this time. Emily managed to keep up. When he came even with a rocky point that extended into the lake, he left the path and broke a new trail through the snow, careful to avoid the rocks. A few minutes later, he and Emily stood in the shadow of a large pine tree, looking out over the ice sheet of Blue Heron Lake. On the shore a mile across the flat expanse to the right, they could see smoke rising from chimneys in the village of Baxter. The islands they could see — Grand Cat, and beyond it Little Cat — remained dark and silent. The sun was working its way west. Its rays touched the top limbs of the trees on Grand Cat's hill, where Emily had found a body the summer before. The golden light refused to bend and hit the gray ice but put a glow on the treetops on the opposite shore.

"Thanks, Nate," Emily said. "This was worth coming out here to see."

They turned back toward the lodge a few minutes later. As they rejoined the path, Nate stopped and held up a hand. A yearling moose stood ten yards away staring at him. Emily moved quietly up beside him and caught her breath. The animal stood as tall as a horse, but thinner, with his long, gangly legs splayed. He eyed them and blew out a breath.

"Look at that!"

"Yeah, and pray his mama's not close by," Nate said.

The young moose let out a bleat and gamboled off into the forest.

"I've missed getting out in the woods and on the lake this winter," Nate said.

"Well, that's what you get for going off to the city, big guy."

"Yeah, right. The academy is in the big city of Vassalboro. I did see some turkeys there last fall, but that's the first moose I've seen since Thanksgiving, when we were driving out here for our first visit with Jeff. Remember?"

"Yeah." Emily's brows drew together in a frown. "Nate, while you were gone with the others this morning, Jeff and Phoebe had a little confrontation."

"About the lodge and the money, like Jeff was saying?"

"Not really. He asked her if she'd gone into that room next to mine last night, and she got all defensive, like he was accusing her of a crime. Later, Jeff told me that when he bought Ian and Phoebe out, they made him pay them top dollar for their shares in the lodge."

Nate couldn't help remembering the things Ian had said during their outing. "And now they're upset because he's making a success of it."

"Yeah, it seems that way. And they're afraid they'll miss out on their share of the mythical treasure."

Nate smiled a little and shook his head. "Don't forget, they grew up with that legend. They probably believe it could happen."

"Phoebe was really upset with Jeff this morning, and it seemed like it was over nothing. Almost like she wanted to pick a fight."

"Maybe she's been brooding on this for a long time," Nate mused.

"Could be. But I know they were planning to stay until tomorrow. I can't believe they stomped off because of the treasure."

"I thought it was odd they packed up and left so suddenly. Especially Ian. But there's quite a bit of resentment on his part, too. I heard enough on the snowmobile outing to realize that. This fight didn't start today, Em."

"I'll bet Phoebe made Ian leave, too, because she didn't want to stay." Emily shivered. "It's getting cold. Let's go in and warm up by the fireplace."

As Nate turned toward the lodge, he heard a shout.

"What was that?"

"It sounded like someone yelling for help." Emily cocked her head and listened.

An unmistakable cry came from the lake. Nate hurried as fast as he could on his snowshoes along the path until he came to a place where the trail neared the shore and the view of the ice was open once again between the trees.

"Someone's out there!"

"It looks like he's fallen through the ice," Emily said.

"Got your cell phone?"

"Yeah. I don't know if it will work here."

"Try!" Nate fumbled at the straps on his snowshoes.

13

The cry came again, fainter.

"I think that's Rocky Vigue!" The bulky figure was low on the surface of the frozen lake. Nate thought he must have broken through and was clinging to the jagged edge of the ice. He looked around for something he could use to help bring him to safety. Strange — Rocky was a lifetime resident of Baxter and knew the folly of going out on the ice in spring. And Nate knew how hard it would be to get the rotund young man out of the frigid lake.

"Rocky, hold on. I'm coming!" Nate wasn't sure Rocky could hear him. To his right he spied a brush pile someone had built on shore, probably for a bonfire. He prayed desperately that in it he'd find a tree limb strong enough to do the job. He ran to the pile and wildly tossed small fir boughs out of the way in search of something larger.

Somewhere in the distance a dog barked.

In spite of his haste, Nate stole a quick glance over his shoulder to see Emily speaking into her cell phone. Good. The rescue unit from the Baxter fire station should be here in ten minutes. But ten minutes might be too late in water that cold.

Baxter's rescue vehicle wasn't a fully equipped ambulance, but the volunteer EMTs would be a great help. Turning back to the brush pile, Nate grabbed hold of a long, thick limb and dragged it from the tangling clutches of the surrounding boughs. He advanced cautiously across the ice, cringing each time it cracked beneath his weight.

It seemed like forever before he approached within ten yards of the hole in the ice, pulling the branch. As the afternoon waned, the temperature was falling. Nate's breath came in painful gulps.

By this time Rocky had stopped yelling, and his thrashing had subsided to a half-hearted waving of his arms each time he bobbed upward. Nate sent up a quick prayer — Lord, don't let him get caught under the ice sheet!

The ice cracked, loud as a gunshot, and he felt it give slightly as a long line ran through it, away from his feet toward the hole. Nate lowered himself to his hands and knees and pushed the limb ahead of him toward Rocky.

"Grab on to this! Rocky, grab on to the branch!"

Rocky's head was barely visible above the surface. It bobbed under again, and Nate's chest tightened. The ice looked to be only about two inches thick where Rocky had fallen through. He slid forward on his belly, pushing the big end of the branch farther over the edge of the hole. Maybe it was long enough to lay completely across the breach, and Rocky could hold on to it and rest. But where was Rocky? Nate raised his head and searched the black water. Was he only a few seconds too late?

A dark object surfaced. The water roiled for a moment, and Rocky opened his blue lips, gasped, coughed, and ducked under.

"Rocky! Come on! I'm here!" Nate was almost at the edge of the hole when a chunk of ice two feet wide gave way beneath his arms. He slid back quickly, getting only the elbows and forearms of his jacket wet. It would do Rocky no good if he ended up in the frigid water with him. The mini iceberg he'd broken off bobbed in the water beside the tree branch.

Rocky was up again, and Nate shoved the branch toward him.

"Grab the branch! Come on, Rocky. You can do it."

Rocky's gloved hands broke the surface and batted at the limb.

"Grab hold. Just hang on."

With a desperate effort, Rocky raised one arm and hooked it over the branch. His head sank beneath the water again, but he held on and quickly came up again choking.

"That's it, buddy. Hold on."

"Nate . . ." Rocky moaned.

Nate felt a sense of relief. At least he was still aware of his surroundings. "Get your other hand on the branch if you can," he shouted again, and this time Rocky did. "Now hold tight."

God, please let me get him out, Nate prayed. And please let him be okay.

The seconds seemed like hours as his efforts to move Rocky threatened instead to drag Nate into the hole. He coaxed Rocky to keep holding on and not to give up.

When Rocky's floating body reached the edge of the ice, Nate called, "Can you hear me, Rocky?"

Rocky nodded slightly. "I'm going to try to pull you up on the ice, but it might break again. Don't panic. Just hold on to the branch. Don't let go, no matter what."

Rocky said nothing.

"Try to slide up on top of the ice, and I'll pull you away from the hole," Nate told him.

"Okay," Rocky gasped.

Nate inched backward and pulled on the branch. He was afraid the freezing water had enervated Rocky so much that he wouldn't be able to help lift his weight. He pulled with all his strength, and the branch moved six inches toward him. Rocky's head was completely out of the water now.

"Come on, Rocky! I've almost got you! Kick if you can. Push yourself up and roll onto the ice." Nate prayed harder and pulled harder, his mind a jumbled mess of frantic thoughts. Adrenaline surged through him, and suddenly the branch slid easily toward him. Rocky lay on the ice, staring at him and panting as his body shivered all over.

"Thank you, Lord," Nate prayed softly. He pulled with all the strength he had left until Rocky was six feet away from the hole. Nate got to his hands and knees and crawled over beside Rocky, who was still coughing and choking, barely able to breathe in the dry, cold air. The ice cracked ominously.

"Rocky, you're going to be okay," Nate said. "There's an ambulance on the way." He wondered if he should get Rocky to shore before the EMTs arrived. He wasn't sure it would be safe for more people to move out onto the ice. He lifted his head and searched the shore for Emily, but he couldn't spot her.

Rocky coughed violently, choking out a few broken words Nate couldn't quite make out.

"What did you say?" He leaned in closer.

"Where's Clinker?" Rocky cried suddenly, his voice stronger than before.

"Clinker?"

"My dog! Where's Clinker? Is he okay?" Rocky's eyes darted back and forth, and he struggled to sit up.

"Easy," Nate said.

A dog's bark echoed across the frozen lake. Nate looked up to see Emily walking gingerly toward them over the ice.

"Stay back," Nate yelled. "The ice could give way again."

She halted fifty feet away. "The rescue unit is coming. And I called Jeff, too. He's bringing a rope and blankets down from the lodge. Rocky, are you okay?"

"I — I — where's Clinker?" His wide eyes were wet with tears, and tiny, frosted water droplets clung to his eyelashes. "Where's my puppy?"

"I saw a dog near the shore over by the

point," Emily said. "Is that your dog, Rocky? He's okay. How can I get him to come to me?"

"Jerky."

"What?" said Nate.

"Beef jerky," Rocky gasped. "In my pocket." His face was bright red from the cold, and his blue lips trembled.

Nate tugged at Rocky's coat, which was stiffening in the cold. Something crackled in the pocket, and he managed to bring out a cellophane package and toss the nearly frozen bag of teriyaki beef strips toward Emily. It skittered across the ice, and she grabbed it.

"All right, I'll find Clinker," said Emily. She turned toward shore. "Clinker!" She started off toward the tree line.

Nate was afraid Rocky was going into shock. He took off his own parka and laid it over Rocky. The cold air immediately began to sap his energy. He leaned close to Rocky and laid a hand on his shoulder. "When did you get a dog?"

"When my parents kicked me out." Rocky pushed his lower lip out.

"Oh." At least he was able to talk.

"I'm fr–fr–freezing, Nate."

"I know. Help is on the way." Nate looked toward shore again and saw Jeff and another figure dashing along the path from the lodge, carrying flashlights.

"Clinker's my best friend." Rocky looked up at him, fresh tears spilling over his eyelids. "Actually, he's my only friend."

"That's not true. You know Emily and I are your friends."

"Okay, then I have three. Nobody else likes me anymore." He stopped to catch his breath again. Every word seemed an effort. " 'Cuz of last summer, and all. But I'm trying to be good now. I've reformed, Nate. I got a job at the video store, and I'm renting my own place down the road from the hunting lodge."

"That's good. People ought to recognize that you want to start over."

"Yeah, well, they don't." He puffed out his cheeks.

In the distance, they could hear Emily calling for the dog. And then, at last, the siren.

"That'll be the rescue unit," said Nate. "You doing okay?"

"Not so good. I can't feel my toes." He scowled deeply. "I can't even feel my feet."

"Jeff is almost here. I'm going to see if he can help me pull you closer to shore. He's got blankets, too. Hang in there, buddy."

Nate crawled several yards from Rocky

before he stood up and called out to Jeff. Lisa had come from the lodge with him. Under Nate's advice, Jeff crawled out to Rocky with a wool blanket. He managed to roll Rocky onto it and drag him farther away from the hole. Lisa gave Nate another blanket to wrap around himself.

When Jeff had pulled Rocky closer to them, Lisa and Nate grabbed the edges of the blanket under him and helped Jeff haul the heavy burden across the ice. By the time they reached shore, the rescue unit had parked as close to them as it could get, and two EMTs were climbing down to the surface of the lake.

In a matter of seconds, the two rescue workers carried a backboard and a medical bag over to where Rocky lay.

"Hey, how we doing?" The first EMT knelt beside Rocky. "My name's Dave. You're Rocky Vigue, aren't you?"

"Yeah," Rocky managed.

"Everything's going to be fine," said Dave. "Ordinarily, I'd examine you here before we move you, but you're awfully cold, so we're going to put you on a stretcher and get you up to the unit as quick as we can. We'll take you right to the hospital, and they'll get you all warmed up. This is Peter." He motioned to the other EMT.

"Rocky, can you tell me your address?" said Peter as Dave enlisted Jeff and Nate to help him get the stretcher down to the ice.

"Forty-five Woodburn Road," said Rocky shakily.

"That's great. I used to go fishing out here when I was a kid. Do you live by yourself?"

"I live with my dog. Nate, where's Clinker?"

"Don't worry about the dog," said Nate. "Emily and I will take care of him until you're feeling better." Emily had liked animals when she was a kid, but he had no idea how she would feel about dog sitting now, or even where they'd keep Clinker, but he felt it was the least he could do.

The four men struggled to get Rocky's heavy form onto the stretcher and over the uneven terrain to the path above. The wheels didn't want to run through the snow, and the shuffle to the waiting vehicle took some time. Once they had Rocky safely in the unit, they gave Nate's coat back to him.

The rescue unit was leaving for the hospital in Aswontee when Emily returned with Clinker nipping at her heels.

"Is Rocky okay?" she called as she snowshoed her way through the woods to intercept Nate, Jeff, and Lisa.

"His body temp was pretty low," Jeff said.

"They're taking him to the hospital in Aswontee, and they think he'll recover completely."

"It's a good thing you and Nate were out here when he broke through," Lisa said.

Jeff shook his head. "I'd have thought Rocky would know better than to go out on the lake this late in the spring, as heavy as he is."

"He was chasing his dog," Nate told them. "I think he was afraid Clinker would fall in, and he ended up going through himself."

"This guy's quite friendly," Emily said, patting the German shepherd mix on the head. "He growled at me at first, but once I broke out the beef jerky, we made friends in a hurry."

Nate reached down to pat Clinker, who responded by lapping his fingers affectionately. "Yuck." Nate wiped his hand on his pants. "I sort of told Rocky we'd take care of him until he's feeling better."

"Great!" Emily rubbed the dog's fur. "Good boy!"

"I thought Rocky was in jail," Lisa said, looking from Jeff to Nate.

Nate shook his head. "He was only in for a few weeks. Suspended sentence, and he made restitution for the thefts." He looked down at Emily, who was still coddling the dog. "Maybe we should drive over and tell Rocky's parents what happened."

"Yeah, Marvin and Truly will probably want to go to the hospital," Emily said.

"I think he'll be all right, Em." Nate paused. "At least partly. But he may need a bit more than treatment for hypothermia. He needs friends right now."

14

Twilight was deepening as Nate drove into the parking lot at the marina and pulled up on the side nearest the house.

"Just a quick stop here," he told Emily. "Jeff's expecting us back at the lodge."

As he went around to open Emily's door, he saw a man emerge from the store. Allison Woods looked out the glass door, waved to Nate, and turned the OPEN sign to CLOSED.

"Hey, there." The man nodded to Nate.

"Mr. Hill. Good to see you."

The man paused. "Aren't you running the marina anymore?"

Nate shook his head and opened the door of the SUV. "No, my mother and I are selling it. That was Allison Woods who waited on you just now. She's worked for us for a couple of years, and she and her husband are interested in buying the business."

As Emily climbed out, Hill walked over

and stood a few feet away from Nate.

"Terrible thing about Mac MacBriarty, isn't it?"

"It sure is." Nate turned slightly to include Emily. He knew this was one introduction she wouldn't want to miss. "Say, I don't believe you've met my fiancée. Emily, this is Ormond Hill."

Emily's smile launched, but she hesitated just a millisecond before extending her hand.

"And this is Emily Gray," Nate finished.

"Mr. Hill," Emily said. "I'm pleased to meet you. Aren't you a registered Maine guide?"

"Yes, I am. Things are a little slow this time of year, but that's all right. I'm tinkering with my outboard." He held up the bag from the marina store. "Got to be ready when fishing season opens."

Nate chuckled. "Right."

Hill looked back at the marina. "Well, things change, don't they? Your dad had this place for a long time."

"Twenty-six years." Nate nodded. His parents had told him many times how they had opened the marina just months before he was born. "We miss him."

"I'll bet. So." Hill looked Emily over more closely. "Getting married, huh?"

"Yes, sir. In August," Emily said.

"What are you going to do now, Nate?" Hill asked.

Nate grinned. "I just graduated from the police academy. I'll be full-time with the county sheriff's department starting Monday."

"Is that right?" Hill nodded genially. "Congratulations."

"Thank you."

Emily cleared her throat. "Mr. Hill, you knew Mac MacBriarty fairly well, didn't you?"

"Oh yes. Mac and I went back a long way."

"I heard you were rivals in business."

Hill chuckled. "You could say that. Oh, Mac and I spent a lot of nights on the trail together. If we met up when we were guiding parties, sometimes we'd share a campfire."

"Um . . ." Emily darted a glance toward Nate then said earnestly, "Mr. Hill, I'm Wiley Gray's daughter. I don't know if you're —"

"Wiley Gray? Of course I remember him! I was at his funeral. And you're his little girl!" Hill shook his head. "Time flies, that's for sure."

"Yes, sir. And I'm a journalist now, just like my mom and dad were."

"You don't say."

"That's right. I'm working with Felicia Chadwick on the *Baxter Journal.*"

Hill's face clouded. "And?"

"I just wondered if you'd like to say anything on the record about Mac. I heard someone say you and he competed for clients."

"Sure, we did. But it was a friendly rivalry." Hill's chin shot out as he sized Emily up. "Look, I don't know what you heard. All of us guides liked to tease each other, but it was part of the camaraderie. If one of Mac's bigwigs came to me the next season, I'd razz him about it, and if one of his clients got a bigger buck than mine did, I'd cuss at him, but it was all good-natured."

"I see. So, would you want to say anything about Mac for the *Journal,* sir? We're putting together a page of reminiscences about him."

His eyes narrowed. "Mac MacBriarty was as good a guide as you could find in these parts."

Emily whipped a small notebook from the pocket of her jacket.

Hill went on, "He knew this whole territory like the back of his hand, and he did even before the days of GPS. You'd never get lost with Mac. He could make good cof-

203

fee. And he never made any guarantees on bagging your limit, but an awfully high percentage of his clients found what they were looking for. Mac just knew where the game was. Fish, too." Hill sighed. "Ayuh, things change."

"Thank you, Mr. Hill," Emily said.

He frowned at her. "Well, I don't like you saying you've heard things, young lady. The police came around a while back, asking me a lot of questions about Mac. It made me think people were insinuating that I might know something about his death. That's ridiculous."

Nate wished strongly that he hadn't introduced Emily to the guide, but it was too late now. She just stood there under his glare, her face pale.

"If you think you can print something in the newspaper like that, forget it. Mac was a friend of mine."

Emily nodded. "I understand. Thank you very much." When Hill got in his truck and drove away, Nate sighed in relief.

"You know, Emily, the newspaper carries a lot of weight in this town. You do need to be careful how you phrase things."

"What's the matter?" Emily asked. "Do you think I'd accuse him of murdering Mac in print?"

"No, but for a minute I was afraid he'd guess you were the one who put Blakeney onto him. You don't want to ruin an innocent person's reputation."

"If he's innocent," she said. "Do you think he was sincere?"

"I do." Inside the SUV, Clinker gave a little bark.

"Hey, fella." Emily opened the rear door and stroked his neck. "Thought we were going to leave you in the car, didn't you?" She looked up at Nate. "You've got leashes in the store, right?"

"Should have. We'd better get some dog food, too."

A minivan drove in, and Nate looked toward it.

"There's Mom. This should only take a minute."

Emily glanced at her watch. "Think we'll get back to the lodge in time to eat dinner with Jeff?"

"Why don't you call him? Tell him not to wait for us if it's inconvenient." Nate walked over to where his mother had parked and opened her door for her.

"I'm sorry, honey," she said as she climbed out of the van. "This won't take a sec. I just need you to sign the intent-to-sell agreement."

"For Allison and Jon?"

Connie shook her head. "For the real estate agency."

"But if we're selling to Jon and Allison, why do we need that? Can't we save the commission and do it ourselves?"

"Bridget said she'd do all the paperwork for us for a flat fee, and I thought it was a reasonable rate. She knows all about that stuff, and it would save us some headaches. We'd know it was done right."

"Okay. Want to go in the house and do it?"

"Allison asked me to give her the contact information for the people I met at the folk art show last fall. I was thinking of ordering in some decorative items, and she liked the sound of it. Let's step into the store, and I'll get that taken care of, too."

Emily joined them, pulling Clinker along by his collar. "Hi, Mrs. Holman."

"Who's this?" Her eyes sparkled as she examined the dog.

"Oh, that's Rocky's dog," Nate said. "I told you on the phone how Rocky fell through the ice."

"Yes, you did," said his mother.

"Well, the reason he was out there on the lake was this mutt. Emily and I are sort of babysitting while Rocky's in the hospital."

"How is he?"

Emily straightened but kept one hand firmly curled about Clinker's collar. "Marvin called us and said the doctor will let him go home tomorrow if everything looks good. His body temp went down a few degrees, but he's really not much worse for the experience."

"Yeah, well, Rocky has a lot of insulation," Nate said.

Connie swatted at him. "You're awful. But praise God you two were out there and were able to help him."

"I know," Emily said. "If Nate hadn't gotten to him when he did, I'm afraid Rocky wouldn't have made it. Mrs. Holman, your son is a hero, and the *Journal* is going to make sure the community knows that."

"My dear girl, don't you think it's time you started calling me Connie?"

Emily gulped. "Uh . . ."

"Or Mom, if you're comfortable with that."

"Thanks." Emily smiled. "I wouldn't mind having an extra mom."

Connie gave her a quick hug. "Come inside with us. I need to give this information to Allison, and we'll sign these papers, and then I'll get out of here."

As they walked toward the marina, Emily

said to Nate, "Jeff says he'll wait and eat dinner with us."

"Great," Nate said. "I'd hate to miss out on Lucille's cooking on our last night at the lodge. And as far as this hero business goes, I wish you and Felicia would play that angle down. It will be embarrassing to face my new boss and coworkers if you brand me a hero. Everyone will expect me to perform perfectly on the job."

Emily shrugged as he opened the marina door. "Okay, I promise we won't use the *H* word in print. But we have to do the story, Nate. It wouldn't be honest not to tell the part you played in the rescue."

"Hi," Allison called as they entered the store. "Just a second, Mrs. H. I'm almost done cashing up." She bent over the counter and punched numbers on a calculator. "Good. Everything balances." She made a note on a slip of paper and slid it into a money bag.

"All done?" Connie asked. "Here's that list of artisans I promised you."

"Oh, thanks! It's exciting to think I'll be ordering merchandise for my own store. A little scary, though."

Connie smiled and patted her arm. "You'll make a roaring success of this place."

"Thanks." Allison looked at the three of

them. "Should I lock up?"

"Go ahead," Nate said. "I'm just going to sign some documents for Mom to take to Bridget, and then we'll vamoose."

"It will start things rolling for you and Jon to become the new owners," Connie said with a smile.

"Great. Jon thinks we'll be okay with the financing. I'll be glad when we get the final word from the bank, though."

"Hey, why don't you go ahead, Allison," Nate said. "I'll lock up before we go."

"Really?"

"Sure. I know the drill." He grinned at her.

"Thanks, Nate."

"Oh, and I'm taking a leash and a bag of dog food. I'll ring it up and put the money in the till. Or do you want to add it to your deposit?"

"Nah, then I'd have to change the deposit slip. Just put it in the cash drawer, and I'll get it in the morning. Night."

Allison went out the front door, and Emily let go of Clinker's collar. He sniffed around the display racks. "Come here, boy," Emily said, striding toward the pet supplies.

"Get whatever you want," Nate said as his mother opened a folder of papers and laid them on the counter.

A moment later, Emily plopped a small bag of dog food and a nylon leash on the counter.

"Need anything else?" Nate asked absently as he skimmed the real estate agent's agreement.

"Not for tonight," Emily said.

Nate scrawled his signature on the document and handed it to his mother. "I guess this is it."

Connie smiled ruefully and looked around the store. "Yeah. We probably won't close for several weeks. That's assuming their financing goes through. You know, I'm glad we're selling."

Nate nodded, but a lump formed in his throat.

"Well, I'll be off," Connie said briskly. "Jared will be wondering what's keeping me. Good night, kids."

"Good night, Mom," Emily said with a saucy smile.

Connie laughed and kissed her cheek. "You're so good for us."

She left the store, and Nate rang up the purchase. Emily pulled the cardboard tag off the leash. Nate walked slowly through the souvenir aisle toward the marine supplies. He could almost see his dad mounting a new outboard motor on the display rack. He pulled in a deep breath.

"Are you okay?" Emily asked from behind him.

"Yeah."

Clinker whined. She stooped and snapped the leash to his collar. "Good dog."

Nate ambled to the back door that opened on the deck leading to the docks. The boats were all out of the water, and off to one side he could see several hulls parked on trailers, wrapped in plastic for the winter. This had been his daily life for twenty-six years.

"Think you can be happy away from here?" Emily asked.

He locked the back door and turned toward her, surprised to find his eyes filling with tears. "Yeah."

"We'll still be right on the lake," she said. "We can keep your boat and maybe a canoe, and have them out at the cottage all summer."

He nodded.

She stepped closer and squeezed his arm. "Honey, are you sure you want to live on the island this summer?"

"Of course I do."

She smiled. "Okay."

Nate shrugged and picked a fishing net off one of the displays. "It will be a hassle getting over to work on time every day, especially if the lake's rough, but it will be worth it. I always envied your family, living on Grand Cat in summer. I thought that must be the coolest place on earth to live."

She laughed. "But you were right here on the same lake."

"I know, but we had to work all summer. You just went out to your cottage and swam and fished and . . . I don't know. I guess I thought you just goofed off for three months solid."

"Well, maybe I did, but Mom and Dad came over to run the paper."

"Oh, yeah. But kids don't think about that stuff." He grinned. "Let's go. I'm hungry, and it's awfully late for dinner."

"Right. Let's not keep Jeff waiting any longer. Emily tugged on the leash. "Come on, Clinker."

Nate turned off all but the security lights. As Emily took Clinker across the dark parking lot toward the SUV, he pivoted and took one last look at the store. *Thank You, Lord. This is the right thing to do.* He closed the door and tried it to be sure it was locked.

When Emily and Nate got back to the lodge, Jeff met them at the door.

"About time, you guys!"

"We're so sorry, Jeff," Emily began.

"I'm kidding. I'm glad you went and told the Vigues what happened in person. Lisa stayed and helped me get dinner. It's all ready." He grinned and led them to the dining room.

Lisa stood by a table set for four near the windows overlooking the lake.

"Welcome back. We've got beef stew and biscuits tonight, with Lucille's famous custard pie and wild blueberry topping for dessert."

"This looks wonderful." Emily surveyed the table set with linen napkins and two burning tapers. In the center of the table, a spray of spruce tips surrounded a wooden carving of a moose.

"It sounds wonderful, too," Nate said. "I'm starved."

Emily laughed. "Let me help you bring in the food, Lisa."

"Oh no," Jeff said. "That's my job. Lisa and I know where everything is. You two just sit down and get comfy."

Emily didn't miss the smile Lisa threw Jeff as the two hurried into the kitchen. "They're cute together," she said.

"Huh?" Nate eyed her keenly. "You mean . . . Jeff and Lisa?"

"Yeah, that's exactly what I mean. I think he likes her, and it's obvious how she feels about him."

Nate frowned, staring at the kitchen door. "Must be a woman thing. I mean, she's attractive and all that, but I didn't notice anything mushy."

"Just watch them while we eat."

Lisa kept her usual quiet demeanor, but a smile of contentment seemed to have taken up residence on her face. Emily couldn't help noticing how often she and Jeff looked at each other as the meal progressed. Jeff's mood seemed lighter than it had that afternoon, though he still had care lines at the corners of his eyes.

After dinner, Jeff suggested a game of Scrabble in his sitting room. Emily eyed Nate eagerly. She could always go for Scrabble, but she wasn't sure about Nate.

"You want to play?" she asked.

"Sure, but Jeff looks tired."

"I'm okay." Jeff opened a cupboard and took out the game box. "If anyone's exhausted tonight, it should be you, Nate. That was quite a rescue you did this afternoon."

Nate flexed his shoulders. "I wasn't sure I could get him out, but I knew he couldn't last long in that water. I just kept praying."

"I'd say God answered," Jeff said.

"Amen." Emily sat down on the sofa, and

Clinker settled on the rug at her feet. Nate sat down beside her, and Lisa took one of the two armchairs. Jeff handed her the box, and she opened it on the coffee table.

"Oh, we forgot one thing," Jeff said.

"What's that?" Emily asked.

"Cocoa."

She laughed. "You don't have to give me cocoa every night. I'm not addicted."

"That's news to me," Nate said. "She buys it in bulk."

Jeff headed for the door. "Go ahead and set up. I'll be back in a few minutes."

"I'll help you." Lisa jumped up and followed. Jeff didn't tell her to stay, Emily noted.

Nate took the bag of letter tiles from the box. "Okay, so I think you're right. I wonder when this happened."

"I'd say it's a recent development. Lisa's been working here at least since last summer, but the chemistry between them seems different. Like maybe Jeff's started looking at her as something more than a great employee." Emily leaned over and kissed Nate's cheek. "I'm so thankful it went all right today. I was afraid you would end up in the lake with Rocky, and there's no way we could have gotten you both out if the ice kept breaking around you."

Nate put his arm around her and pulled her close for a moment. "I had the same thought. But God was merciful."

"Yes."

He kissed her then turned back to setting up the game. Emily watched him with a new sense of life's fragility. *Thank You, Lord, for keeping him safe and for letting him rescue Rocky.* Nate glanced over and winked at her. *And for bringing us back together after seven years apart.* It was all God's timing, she knew. And she would always be grateful.

"I love you," she said.

"Ditto. Even if you are about to trounce me and Jeff royally at this game. I don't know about Lisa."

"Want me to let you win?"

"Don't you dare. I'll get back at you next time we play Rook."

"I don't think I've seen a Rook game since high school."

"Great. I'll have an even better chance of beating you. Our old set is over at the house somewhere."

"Snowshoeing isn't enough? You want to humiliate me."

"That's right."

They were both laughing when Jeff came in with the tray of steaming mugs. Lisa followed with a cut glass bowl of marshmallows.

Lisa sat down and smiled at Emily. "I'll bet you're really good at this, since you're a writer."

"Don't listen to her," Jeff said. "Lisa's the champ around here."

Nate chuckled. "That's great. Emily will have some real competition for a change."

The game progressed with the women leading the men by an ever-widening margin amid laughter and talk about summer plans.

An hour later, Nate yawned as Emily added their final scores.

"Who won?" Jeff asked.

"Well, I don't want to brag, but . . ."

"Of course you do." Nate snatched the paper from her hand. "Ew. Did you have to beat us by so much?"

"Yes."

Nate blinked at the paper; then he leveled his gaze at Lisa. "You almost beat her, you know. That makes me feel a little bit better. Of course, I came in last."

Jeff leaned back in his chair. "If you'd made daze instead of date, you could have evened the score."

"I never can think of z words." Nate lifted the board and bent it enough to funnel the tiles into the bag.

"Rematch?" Jeff asked.

"I'm too tired to pull that off again," Emily said.

"Me, too," said Lisa.

Nate covered the box and stood up. "Thanks, Jeff. That was a lot of fun."

"Hey, I'm glad you guys stayed. I was feeling a little low after Phoebe and Kent and Ian left. And I hardly ever get to sit down and do something like this with anyone."

Emily thought it was a little sad that Jeff hadn't pulled out the Scrabble game the night before, while his siblings were there, and even sadder that they were angry with Jeff over a hypothetical treasure that no one would ever find.

"Well, I enjoyed it a lot, and not just because I won. Lisa, I'm glad you stayed."

"Thanks." Lisa glanced at Jeff. "It was fun."

Emily stood, and Clinker gave a little woof and jumped to his feet.

"You baby. You don't want us to leave you alone, do you?" She bent to pat him. "Do you want to sleep in my room tonight?"

"Uh, maybe you should ask Jeff," Nate said.

Emily turned to their host with a rueful smile. "I'm sorry, Jeff. If you don't allow pets in the rooms, it's okay. We can fix him up down here."

"No, it's fine," Jeff said. "Just don't let him up on the new bedding, okay?"

"You got it. Come on, fella."

As they left the room, Emily heard Jeff say to Lisa, "I can drive you home if you want."

Clinker followed her and Nate eagerly into the lobby and leaped up the stairs beside her. He seemed content to settle on the carpet beside her bed. Emily realized how tired she was from the fresh air and exertion of the day. She quickly undressed and climbed into bed.

"Good night, Clinker."

She rolled over and drifted into sleep.

Suddenly she woke up. Clinker barked frantically. She turned on the lamp and glanced at the clock. It said 2:00 a.m.

"What is it, boy?"

Clinker continued his barking, and she realized a high-pitched beeping came from somewhere outside her room.

Emily climbed out of bed and hurried to the door. As the scent of smoke hit her nostrils, she caught her breath. She put a hand on the wooden panel of the door, but it didn't feel hot, so she opened it.

The hall was thick with smoke.

15

Frantic pounding on his bedroom door pulled Nate from a deep sleep.

"Nathan! Wake up! We've got a fire!"

He sprang out of bed and grabbed his jeans. "I'm coming, Em!" Even as he said it, the stench of smoke filled his nostrils. He grabbed his cell phone from the nightstand, snagged his shirt from the chair, ran to the door, and threw the dead bolt. Emily stood in the hazy hallway, a ghost in pale pajamas, with Rocky's mongrel pressing against her and whining. Her flashlight beam cut across the swirls of smoke.

"Go downstairs, Emily. Take the dog with you." Nate coughed and opened his phone.

"I'm not leaving without you." Emily tugged Clinker's collar and pulled the dog toward her. She moved toward the stairs but paused when Nate lagged behind.

"Did you call the fire department?" he asked, pushing 911 as he spoke. The dog whined again.

"No. Come on! We've got to tell Jeff and get out of the lodge!"

Nate tried not to let Emily's stubbornness frustrate him. She wants to help, he told himself. He let her pull him toward the stairs.

The phone rang only twice before someone picked up. "Baxter Fire Department."

"This is Nate Holman. We have a fire at the hunting lodge on Woodburn Road."

Clinker kept pace, whining constantly, now and then interspersing sharp barks of warning.

"It's okay, Clinker," Emily said, but her voice held a tinge of fear. "We're going to get out."

Nate listened to the dispatcher and answered questions as quickly as possible as they navigated the stairs and made their way toward Jeff's suite. Smoke swirled around them.

"We've got a truck and an ambulance on the way now," said the dispatcher.

"Great, thanks!" Nate closed his phone and tried the door to Jeff's apartment. Another smoke alarm overhead screeched. The door wasn't locked, so he advanced into the sitting room and pounded on the door to the bedroom. "Jeff, wake up! There's a fire! Wake up!"

Emily was right on his heels. "The smoke's worse down here." She coughed and gasped for breath.

"I know." Nate heard panic in his own voice. "Go on outside now. Take the dog with you." He tried the doorknob and threw the bedroom door open.

Jeff staggered toward him, bleary-eyed and confused. "What's going on?"

"Fire," said Nate. "We have to get out."

Jeff's eyes widened in disbelief. "No! This is crazy!" He grabbed his wallet and a sweatshirt from his dresser. "Did you call the fire department?" He pulled the sweatshirt on over his head as they hurried across his sitting room.

"Yes," said Nate. "They're on their way." He looked over his shoulder and saw Emily hovering in the doorway. As usual, she was too stubborn to listen to reason.

"Well, let's get out of here." Jeff followed them out into the lobby.

Emily guided Clinker to the front door, pulling at his collar. Where was the new leash, Nate wondered. He thrust the door open, and they were met with a blast of frigid air. He hesitated. "Maybe we should have grabbed coats —"

"Where's Lisa?" Jeff asked.

Nate stared at him. "I thought you took her home."

Jeff's face blanched. "No, she decided to stay because it was so late. She's up in the staff quarters." He turned and ran back into his room and grabbed the phone.

Nate whirled. "Emily, take the dog and go out! Now!" He coughed. The smoke was increasing.

Jeff threw the receiver down. "The phone's dead. I've got to run up and get her."

"No!" Nate grabbed his arm. "Let's just get outside. Does she have a cell phone?"

"Yeah, she got it for Christmas."

"We'll call her from outside." Nate pushed him across the smoke-filled lobby. They burst into the fresh air, and Nate dragged his friend down the steps to where Emily waited. Jeff was already pushing buttons on his cell phone.

Emily reached for Nate, and he put his arm around her. "What about Lisa?"

"Jeff's trying to call her." *Answer the cell phone,* Nate thought as he watched Jeff listening. Then he slipped into prayer mode. *God, please let Lisa hear the phone and wake up. Please protect her.*

Jeff let his hand drop to his side. "It went straight to voice mail."

"She has it off," said Emily. "What are we

going to do?"

"What room is she in?" Nate asked.

"Around the back."

"Could we get her out a window?"

Jeff inhaled sharply, his gaze darting about the yard. "Maybe. There's a lower roof below, over the kitchen."

Nate pressed his key ring into Emily's hand. "Get in the car, Em. Move it away from the building."

Jeff was already running around the corner of the lodge, and Nate followed him. Jeff pointed up to the third-story window on the end. "That's her room. The last two windows."

"Do you have a ladder?"

"Yeah, but it would take time to get it, and it's not that tall, anyway.

Desperate times call for desperate measures, Nate thought. He looked at Jeff. "Throw rocks at the windows? Do you mind if we break the glass?"

Jeff nodded. "Let's do it."

Nate looked down at his feet and kicked at the snow until pebbles and bits of gravel began to surface. Jeff followed his lead and scrambled for stones.

When he'd found one large enough, Nate took it in his hand and aimed for the third-story window. Just like playing baseball, he thought. He swung the rock forward and released it.

Thunk! It slammed against the wall inches from the glass.

He hefted another rock. This time his aim was true. The rock soared through the window, smashing the glass. "If that doesn't wake her up, I don't know what will." Nate watched the windows for any sign of movement.

Emily came tearing around the corner. "I hear sirens."

Nate heard them, too, but he kept his eyes on the lodge, waiting for a sign that Lisa had woken. Jeff threw a rock and succeeded in breaking the other window. Nate hefted a larger one and hesitated. He didn't want to strike Lisa if she was coming to the window.

The sirens wailed louder as Lisa lifted the shattered window and stuck her head outside. "Jeff, is that you? What's going on?"

Nate ran out to the parking area.

"We've got a woman on the third story, around the back."

The firemen immediately grasped the situation and drove the ladder truck across the snowy lawn and up near the back of the building. By the time it was in position, Lisa had climbed out the window and lowered herself to the kitchen roof. The tanker truck pulled up, and men leaped off it and started unrolling the fire hose.

The fire chief approached Jeff. "Anyone else inside?"

Jeff shook his head. "Just Lisa, and it looks like she's okay."

The chief nodded and glanced toward where two of his men were assisting Lisa down the ladder.

"You'd better move that other car out front. Then you folks had better get into the vehicles and keep warm. Stay out of the way and let my men do their job."

"You got it," Nate said.

Jeff waited at the bottom of the ladder. When Lisa reached the ground, he embraced her.

"Are you okay?"

"Yes, but I'm cold."

"Come on!" Jeff hurried her around to the front of the lodge. Nate and Emily followed.

The rescue unit pulled in, and the EMTs brought them a couple of blankets. Emily took one and wrapped it around Lisa.

"What happened, anyway?" Lisa asked as Emily led her toward Nate's SUV.

"We don't know, except we woke up to all that smoke. I'm sorry we didn't alert you sooner. Nate and I didn't realize you were still here until after we'd woken Jeff up."

Lisa turned her head aside and coughed.

"Are you all right?" Emily asked.

"Yeah, I think so. My throat's on fire, but the rest of me is freezing."

"I'll see if the EMTs have any bottled water. You'd better get into one of the cars. Oh, and if you get in Nate's, be aware that there's a dog inside. He's friendly, though."

Emily saw Nate and Jeff coming toward them. She knew Lisa would be in good hands, so she squeezed her shoulder and hurried toward the rescue unit.

"Do you have any water?" she asked one of the EMTs. "Lisa's throat is pretty scratchy from the smoke. I guess we're all pretty dry."

"Sure. You should all let us check you over. Did you inhale much smoke?" the man asked.

"Some, while we were getting out. But I feel a lot better now."

He nodded and handed her two water bottles. "I'll come with you and check on the others." He grabbed two more bottles and walked with her to Nate's vehicle. Jeff had also moved his car, but he and Lisa joined them beside the SUV.

When the EMT had examined them all

and taken their vital signs, he left them alone. More volunteer firefighters pulled up in cars and pickups, and the fire chief gave them orders. Emily huddled with Lisa and Clinker in the backseat of Nate's vehicle. Nate sat in front, but Jeff insisted on standing outside, a few yards closer to the lodge, watching every move the firefighters made.

"I'm really sad this happened to Jeff," Lisa said.

Nate nodded. "I know. Seems like awfully bad timing."

"And he spent all that money remodeling and redecorating," Emily said.

"I wonder if the firemen have put out the fire." Lisa leaned forward to see better.

"I never did see much of a blaze," Nate said. "Lots of smoke, though."

Emily stroked Clinker's silky neck. "You are some dog. Seems to me there's more than one hero in this town."

"Is that Rocky's mutt?" Lisa asked.

"Yeah. He woke me up, or we might all still be inside."

Lisa reached over to pat him. "What a good dog! We'll have to tell Rocky. He'll be so proud."

"I'll do better than that," Emily said. "His picture will be on the front page of Tuesday's *Journal*."

"There's the fire chief," Nate said. He opened his door and got out, standing in the angle it formed with the car. Emily could hear the chief's voice clearly.

"You're fortunate, Lewis. We think the blaze is out, but we won't leave until we're absolutely certain. The fire was confined to a hallway and pantry at the back of the kitchen, and only a small area was actually damaged by flames. The smoke damage will be another story. It'll take a lot of time and effort to get rid of the smell and grime."

"Hey, I'm just glad it wasn't more serious," Jeff said. "Twenty minutes ago, I was sure this whole place was going up in flames."

The chief shook his head. "Well, you've got your work cut out for you."

16

Arctic air whooshed in as Emily threw open the window of room 10, the last of Lakeview Lodge's guest rooms. The rising sun threw a golden sheen over the ice on the lake. Emily filled her lungs with fresh air.

"It's freezing in here," Lisa said.

"I know, but you'll never get rid of the smoke smell if you don't air everything out right away." Emily turned away from the window. "It's supposed to get up above forty today, so the pipes won't freeze if Jeff leaves everything open all day. But you'll need to close it up before sunset and get the heat on in these rooms again."

Lisa pulled the comforter and sheets off the bed and sank onto the mattress with a sigh. "Do you think it will work and everything will smell fresh again before Friday?"

"I sure hope so."

"And we just made all these beds up."

"I know, but if you don't wash the sheets

and air the comforters, the smell will linger. I'm sorry you have to do all that work."

Lisa stood up with a grim smile. "Sarah and Ginnie promised to come over right after lunch and help me with the laundry."

"Then you'd better get a few hours' sleep."

"You, too."

Emily shrugged. "I think Nate and I are going to go home, eat breakfast, get showered and changed, and go to church."

"Good thing you've got clothes somewhere else that don't smell like smoke. Jeff's whole wardrobe is probably ruined. His room is close to where the fire started." Lisa stooped to gather the soiled linens.

Emily wadded up the white comforter. Tiny particles of soot gave it a gray tinge. "Most of his things will probably be okay once they're washed. But the damage in the kitchen will be harder to fix."

"Jeff's going to see if the electrician can come today, even though it's Sunday." Lisa led the way into the hallway and stuffed the sheets and towels from room 10 into the laundry chute. She turned to take the comforter from Emily. "Here, I'll take that and add it to the pile for the dry cleaner."

"Nate and I can take a load into town, if that will help," Emily said.

"The dry cleaner won't be open today,

and you don't want to carry smoky blankets and drapes around with you in Nate's vehicle until tomorrow."

"I'll see what Jeff thinks. Maybe the cleaners will open up specially for him once they know about the fire."

Nate came up the stairs. "How are you ladies doing?"

"We've got all the textiles except the rugs out of the guest rooms," Lisa said. "I'll go up to the staff quarters and start there. I don't think the smoke was as bad upstairs, and I opened the windows earlier. Of course, it may be worse than I think. I'm sure I've gotten used to the smell."

Nate nodded. "The fire marshal says they probably won't let Jeff into the kitchen today, so he's ordering breakfast in for you from the Lumberjack. Sam, Royce, and Lucille are all coming to help you."

"Great," Lisa said. "Ginnie and Sarah will come later."

"Some other people may come to help once the word gets out," Emily said.

"Yeah, we'll tell everyone at church," Nate agreed. "It wouldn't surprise me if you had a whole crew later on."

"I don't know how much good it will do until we get the electricity and water back." Lisa shook her head. "Have they said what started it?"

"Not yet. It seems to have started in the hallway between the kitchen and the back door."

"I sure hope it's not a problem in the new wiring," Emily said.

"Me, too."

Lisa looked at her watch. "You two had better get moving if you plan to get cleaned up in time for church."

Nate chuckled. "Yeah, if my face is as filthy as Emily's, it may take awhile."

In the SUV on the drive in to Baxter, Emily sat back and thought about all that had happened that night. Clinker whined in the backseat.

"I still smell smoke," Nate said as he pulled into Felicia's driveway.

"It's our clothes and our hair," Emily said. "Make sure you hang out the things in your luggage, too, and leave your duffel bag out on the deck in the breeze."

"I wish I could have done more for Jeff." Nate sighed and pulled the keys from the ignition. "He is so discouraged."

"I don't blame him. Do you think we should have stayed longer?"

Nate frowned then shook his head. "We're both working tomorrow, and Mom wanted me to help her this afternoon. She needs to get a start on inventorying the store so she can turn it over to Jon and Allison after the closing."

"Well, let's at least see if the church people can do something to help Jeff. He's got guests coming in five days, and I'm not sure that's enough time to put things back together and get rid of the smoke."

"Yeah." Nate got out and came around to open her door then released Clinker from the backseat. The dog jumped out onto the pavement, and Nate handed Emily the end of the leash. He reached inside for her overnight bag and computer case. "I'll bring these in for you."

"Thanks. Felicia will probably shoot me when she hears there was a fire at the lodge and I didn't call her."

"She couldn't have done anything, and you'll do the story for her."

Emily shrugged. "I know, but I forgot to take any pictures. She'll want to know why."

"Why didn't you?"

"I guess I could have clicked some on my cell phone after the fire trucks got there. I think I was too close to it emotionally. I was so worried about Lisa, I didn't think to document her rescue. I did take a couple this morning of her hanging drapes out on the line to air."

"Yeah, well, I'm not sure why I slept through that smoke alarm, but I'm thankful God sent that mutt along to wake you up when he did." Nate reached down to pat Clinker on the head. "Thanks for getting us up, buddy."

Emily smiled wearily. "I'd kiss you if you weren't so grubby."

"Hold on." Nate reached out with one soot-blackened finger and touched the tip of her nose.

"What?"

"You had a clean spot."

She laughed. "Go get cleaned up, and I'll see you in an hour."

At noon, Nate walked out of the church beside Emily, feeling refreshed and very thankful. Already his mother was organizing church volunteers to help with the cleanup at the lodge and take food to the workers.

At the door, he shook his stepfather's hand.

"I'm glad you kids are all right," Pastor Phillips said.

"God was truly merciful," Nate said. "It could have gotten so much worse in a hurry."

"You said Jeff didn't lose any personal possessions?"

"Not unless the smoke wrecked his books and things. I don't know about his sofa and other furniture in his suite."

"The insurance company should replace any that he can't salvage," Emily said.

Nate sighed. "Yeah, we just don't know yet. I don't think anything actually burned except a couple of walls and a few items in the kitchen. But the smoke — that was bad. I guess we'll have a better idea what can be saved after the fire marshal is done with his investigation. He may have to replace the bedding, curtains, rugs, all that stuff. And he's supposed to open on Friday."

"Well, we'll keep Jeff in prayer. I'll go out for a few hours tomorrow and see if I can help him out."

"I'm sure Jeff will appreciate that," Nate said.

"Are you having lunch with us?" the pastor asked.

Nate looked at Emily.

"Sure," she said.

Pastor Phillips nodded. "Great. Head on over to the house if you want. Connie and I will be along in a few minutes."

Nate took Emily's hand and walked across the yard toward the parsonage. The snow was melting, and a patch of grass showed on the church lawn. He paused on the front stoop and reached up under the decorative bracket on the left side. He could reach the hidden spare key without even stretching.

His phone rang, and he passed the key to Emily.

"Hello?"

"Nate, it's Jeff. I hate to ask you, but can you come back out here?"

Nate looked at Emily and tried to telegraph his concern to her. "Sure, Jeff. What's up?"

"It's the fire marshal. He thinks the fire was arson."

"Isn't this awful?" Sarah Walsh, one of the lodge's chambermaids, met Nate and Emily at the door.

"It sure is," Nate agreed.

"Jeff's in his office. He asked me to tell you to come right in."

"Is your sister here, too?" Emily asked, shrugging out of her coat.

"She was here, and our mom came over, too. They took a huge pile of laundry to the Laundromat in Aswontee, but there's going to be a lot more."

"Did you folks get some lunch?" Nate asked.

Sarah grinned. "Yes, the Lumberjack sent

two large pizzas and a case of cold drinks gratis."

"That's great," Emily said. "Mrs. Phillips is organizing work crews to come and help whenever Jeff is ready for them. She's going to bring supper over tonight, with enough food for at least ten people."

"Wow, that's terrific. Everyone's being so nice. And Lisa told me how you guys and Jeff woke her up and got her out. You all could have suffocated in the smoke. Although the third-floor rooms don't look too bad. Most of them were closed up, and I think a good airing will be all they need."

Emily winced. "Too bad the guys had to break the windows in Lisa's room."

"Maybe some of the men from church can fix those," Nate said.

Sarah left them, and they went to the doorway of Jeff's office. He was slumped in his swivel chair, staring at a pile of papers on the desktop.

"Hey, Jeff," Nate said.

Jeff raised his chin then jumped up from the chair. "Hi. Thanks for coming! I realized after I called that I shouldn't have dumped this on you."

"No, it's fine." Nate pulled a chair out from the wall for Emily, and Jeff scurried to move books from another one for Nate.

"So, what did you learn about the fire?" Emily asked when they were seated.

Jeff sighed and picked up the top sheet of paper from his stack. "The fire marshal is sure someone set the fire deliberately. Apparently it was started in a big plastic trash can in the hallway between the kitchen and back door."

Nate nodded, picturing the spot.

"But see, that's not right," Jeff said.

"What do you mean?" Nate asked.

"We never keep that trash can there. It's always in the kitchen. Lucille or one of her kitchen helpers empties it every day when we have guests staying here. Sometimes I do it myself."

"Where does the trash go?" Emily asked.

"Into the Dumpster outside. It's across the back parking area, beside the equipment shed. But the fire marshal says the can was in the hallway last night, and someone put a match to the trash. The fire put off a lot of smoke, and it set off the smoke alarms. He said it probably set off the ones in the kitchen within seconds, and the ones upstairs within a couple of minutes." Jeff rubbed the back of his neck. "I can't believe I slept through all that."

"Don't you have a smoke alarm in your suite?" Nate asked.

"No, but there's one in the hallway outside my sitting room."

"Yeah, that one was working."

Jeff shrugged. "I was pretty tired last night. I guess with two closed doors between me and the alarm, it wasn't enough to get through to me. Maybe I should put one right over my bed."

"You must be exhausted now," Emily said.

Nate nodded. "You really need to get some rest, Jeff."

"How can I rest with all this going on?" He sighed. "I think I'll be able to sleep here tonight, although it still stinks. I'm going to have to take out the carpet in here and all the rugs in the lobby and the guest rooms, I'm afraid."

"At least you have wood floors in most of the lodge," Nate said. "No wall-to-wall carpeting."

"Just in here and the library. Anyway, the fire marshal said Clinker probably saved us from a big dose of smoke inhalation. He must have heard the first smoke alarms go off and started barking before it got too thick."

"So, was the fire confined to the trash can?" Nate asked.

"No. It must have smoldered for a while. Remember how we didn't see any flames through the windows at first? I'm not sure what was in the can. Lucille had emptied it in the afternoon, but there was probably some trash — waste from food preparation, packaging, that sort of stuff."

"Kitchen trash," said Emily.

"Yeah. But maybe whoever started it put something else in to make it smoke a lot. Anyway, eventually it must have gotten really hot and the plastic trash can started melting, and that added to the fumes."

"So it didn't spread fast at first," Emily said.

"Right. But I guess eventually it must have eaten into the wall and shorted out the wiring. The power was out before the fire department got here."

"Yes, and the phones weren't working."

"Are they going to let you get some repairmen in here tomorrow?" Nate asked.

"I don't know. The fire marshal told me that I can set it up, but I can't touch anything in the area of the fire until he gives the word. He taped off the hallway, and we can't go down there or in the kitchen." Jeff raked a hand through his hair. "I just don't know if we'll be able to get things in shape and be ready to serve meals by Friday."

Nate gritted his teeth as he considered all that Jeff had told him. It was obvious that the fire marshal was treating Jeff as a suspect in the arson. But Jeff either had not realized that or was trying to avoid thinking about it.

"Is the fire marshal still here?" he asked.

"I think so. He was still taking samples or something like that a half hour ago. But he told me I had to go away and let him do his job, so I came out here and called you."

Emily had been very quiet, and Nate reached over to squeeze her hand. "What are you thinking?" he asked.

She smiled up at him with a little shrug. "I'm not sure we can help, but I was thinking that maybe you could talk to the officer. He might give you a professional report and a better idea of what the time frame will be for his investigation."

Nate nodded. "I'll give it a whirl. It's probably best if you two stay here, though."

He walked slowly around the corner to the hallway that led to the kitchen, but halfway there he encountered yellow crime scene tape. A man was kneeling on the floor next to the wall near the back door, using a tape measure. Nate leaned over the yellow tape and peered through the open doorway to the kitchen. Inside he could see another man looking at the huge commercial cookstove.

Nate cleared his throat. "Excuse me."

The man in the hallway looked toward him. "Yes?"

"I'm Nate Holman. I'm a sheriff's deputy, but I'm not on duty right now. I was wondering if I could talk to the fire marshal."

The man rose and walked toward him. "I'm Scott James. How can I help you?"

"Well, sir, J — the owner tells me that you've ruled this an arson."

"No doubt," James said.

Nate nodded. "Have you found any evidence as to who committed the act?"

James sighed and stretched his long arms. "So far the clues are pretty slim, but I haven't finished my investigation yet."

"So, do you have an idea how long it will be before you reach some conclusions?"

"Not really. We're looking at sort of a nuisance fire. Someone wanted to make a lot of smoke. They tossed a wool coat into the trash can. Lots of smoke from that."

Nate blinked and peered down the hallway. "Is that mess what's left of the trash can?"

"Yup."

"It's near the coat rack. You don't think the coat fell in after the fire started?"

"Nope. It's close, but not that close."

"And the fire burned into the wall and

shorted out the electricity?" Nate asked.

"I didn't say that."

Nate waited, watching the man's face.

At last James sighed. "I've got more investigating to do, but I'll tell you one thing: We'll be looking hard at the owner."

17

Nate found Jeff and Emily still seated in the office. His friend looked up, a hint of hopefulness in his expression. "So, what did he tell you?"

Nate hesitated. He sat down next to Emily. Would it be better to tell Jeff exactly what he'd learned from the fire marshal or to answer vaguely? In the end he figured Jeff should be as prepared as possible to face a new onslaught of suspicion.

"Basically he said they think you might be the one who started the fire."

Emily's face flushed. "Oh, that makes me mad! As if Jeff would pay top dollar to fix this place up and then turn around and destroy his own efforts."

"I know," said Nate, "but they don't see it that way. It's the fire marshal's job to investigate every possible angle. And they do usually look at the property owner first in an arson case."

"Yes, but assuming that Jeff has committed arson isn't exactly what I'd call investigating every angle."

Jeff sighed. "I can't really say I'm surprised. In fact, at this point I wouldn't be surprised if I were suddenly accused of causing a devastating mud slide in Timbuktu." His mouth formed a wry, half-hearted smile. "It's one thing after another."

"Emily and I are praying for you regularly." Nate sat down. "I know that sounds trite, but we genuinely care, and we believe God does, too. It may seem like it's not helping, but I'm confident God has reasons for everything that's going on."

"I wish I had your confidence," said Jeff. "But I do appreciate the prayers."

There was silence for a minute or two. Nate wondered whether to pursue the topic. He felt he should say something else to encourage Jeff.

Emily said, "I told Jeff we'd take a load of bedding over to the Laundromat. I wish there was something more we could do."

"No, it's okay," said Jeff. "You've been great. You've done a lot, and I can't expect you to drop everything for me. Some of the staff have agreed to do overtime to get the place in shape." He looked up with a lopsided smile. "Lisa's been . . . she's been terrific. She's been working all day. And the Walsh girls and their mom are pitching in."

"That's good," said Nate.

"But I still don't have power or water." Jeff shook his head. "This sure beats all. If I'd known how much trouble this place would cause me, I never would have bought out my brother and sister."

"But it's only been the past six months," Emily said. "I guess your insurance won't pay for this?"

"Not a chance," said Nate. "Not until the arson case is resolved, or at least until Jeff is exonerated."

Jeff huffed out a short breath. "Like I said, one thing after another. First they think I killed Mac, and now they have me pegged as an arsonist. Someone must hate me to set me up this badly. But who?"

Nate gritted his teeth. The thought had occurred to him, but he couldn't believe Jeff's siblings would do such a cruel thing, and he couldn't think of anyone else who could benefit from doing it. It seemed more likely that the fire wasn't connected to Mac's death. "I don't know, Jeff."

"Would you mind if we prayed now?" Emily asked tentatively.

"It couldn't hurt," Jeff said. "It's going to take a lot to get this place fixed up again before Friday, and I could use all the help I can get."

They bowed their heads, and Emily started to pray.

"Dear God, we come to You humbled by Your power, Your love, and Your sovereignty. We know that You are in control of everything, even the things we don't understand. I ask that You would give Jeff faith, peace, and strength as he puts things back in order here at the lodge. And please clear up the mystery surrounding the fire soon."

"Amen," said Nate. He followed her prayer with a similar plea for everything to work out quickly and smoothly. He opened his eyes and was about to say something when he realized Jeff still had his head bowed.

"God, help me," he said. "Just help me out."

That evening, Felicia joined Nate and Emily in folding the laundry they'd done for Jeff.

"I've never seen such a run of bad luck before," Felicia said, shaking her head. "Jeff's had more than his share, for certain."

"I know." Emily folded a towel and laid it on the stack she'd started. "Break-ins and people poking around at night and a nuisance fire with all this smoke damage."

"And somewhere in there Mac MacBriarty gets murdered," Nate added.

"Yeah." Emily reached for another bath towel. "That's what I don't understand. The motive. I mean, who could possibly benefit from Mac's death?"

"Not the ex-wife?" Felicia asked.

Emily shook her head. "Mac didn't have much of an estate. The way I see it, he was worth more to Shannon alive than dead. He kept up his child support payments."

"Well, your theory about him and Ormond Hill being enemies hasn't gone anywhere," Nate said.

"I know. I don't really think Mr. Hill killed him. At least we know the police questioned him."

"After I start duty tomorrow, maybe I can pick up some news," Nate offered, "although I'm not sure how much the state police share with the county sheriff's department."

"This fire . . ." Emily absently smoothed the towel. "It can't have anything to do with the murder, can it? And the break-ins. I can understand someone wanting to rob the lodge, but burn it down?"

"And if they really wanted to burn it flat, why didn't they use a little accelerant?"

Nate asked. "That fire was definitely fishy. Do you think Jeff could be right, and someone just has it in for him?"

"Well, I'm going to write a story for Tuesday's paper about the cleaning company Jeff found in Bangor," Felicia said. "They make it sound like they can get rid of the odors and soot in just a few days."

"I hope they can." Emily laid down the towel and reached for another. "And I'm doing the story about how all the church and community people have helped. If Jeff is able to open Friday, it will be because of all the people who made it happen."

"And they think we New Englanders are cold and unfeeling." Felicia snapped a pillowcase and began to fold it. "Oh, Emily, don't forget you're covering the selectmen's meeting in Aswontee this week. I know you hate those budget meetings, but —"

"But you're making me go anyway," Emily said. "You New Englanders are so cold and unfeeling."

About midday on Monday, Nate rapped on the screen door of Rocky's shabby little house, Clinker's leash grasped in his other hand. The dog wagged his tale expectantly.

"Hi, Nate." Rocky opened the inside door for him. "You brought Clinker back!"

"Yes, Emily called me and said you were released from the hospital this morning." Clinker bounded past Nate into Rocky's kitchen and immediately jumped up to lick his master's face.

"Hiya, boy!" Rocky beamed. "Good dog, Clinker. I've got some puppy treats for you. Nate, you want anything? People food, I mean. I have some Pop-Tarts if you're hungry."

"That's okay, Rocky. I've had lunch, and I start work at three, but I'm trying to squeeze in a quick trip out to the lodge to check up on things. But thanks for the offer."

Rocky looked up from the bag of dog biscuits he was tearing open. Clinker sat poised at his feet, waiting patiently for his treat. "Oh, yeah, I heard about the fire. Was it really bad?"

"Not too bad," said Nate. "No one was hurt or anything. But it did something to the wiring, and there's a lot of smoke damage to take care of. Jeff's pretty depressed about it."

"Yeah, I'll bet," said Rocky. He held a treat out to Clinker. "Maybe I can help."

Clinker happily grabbed the treat from Rocky's hand and began to crunch it up.

"Oh, I don't know, Rocky. I think you should take it easy."

"I've been taking it easy, Nate. What do you think I was doing in the hospital, push-ups?"

Nate laughed. "Okay, you got me there. If you want to go, put your shoes on."

"All right! Just let me get my sneakers and a coat."

Nate waited in the kitchen, and a few seconds later Rocky returned dressed for the outdoors in a heavy green coat, a brown and red striped scarf, and red hat and mittens. His heavy clothing added more bulk than usual to his already hefty form. In his hand he carried what looked like a wadded-up sweater.

"This is Clinker's sweater," Rocky explained. He knelt and pulled it on over Clinker's front paws and head. "The doc said we should bundle up when we go outside."

Nate nodded, trying to keep a straight face as he watched. Clinker's red sweater was a close match to Rocky's mittens and hat.

After Rocky locked the door, they piled into Nate's truck and drove the short distance to the lodge. Jeff waved to them from the front porch when they arrived. He was talking to a man in coveralls.

"Hey, Jeff!" Nate called as he got out of the truck. "Brought a friend with me."

"Howdy, Rocky," said Jeff. "Good to see you on your feet."

"Thanks." Rocky smiled. "Clinker and I decided to come help out."

"Thank you." Jeff seemed unsure of what to say then, but he eyed Clinker with great interest. "That's a snazzy-looking outfit your dog has."

Rocky grinned and patted Clinker's head.

The man wearing coveralls nodded at Jeff and said, "All right, I'll see you tomorrow."

"Yeah, thanks for coming so quickly," Jeff said.

The man walked down the steps and got into a pickup truck with a custom cap on the back. Nate noted the words Oliver Electric on the door. "Well, let's not stand outside in the cold," Jeff said. "Not that it's that much warmer inside with all the windows open." He led them to the dining room. "Nate, your mom brought tons of stuff over for the crew. Sandwiches, chips, veggies, brownies. Enough to feed an army."

"Brownies?" Rocky licked his lips.

"Help yourself," said Jeff. He motioned toward the table, where plastic storage containers were spread, and Rocky went over to peruse the food.

"No thanks," said Nate. "I can't stay, but I thought I'd see how things are going."

"Well, the fire marshal promised to be done by five," said Jeff.

"Really? That's good news. Then you can get moving on the repairs."

"And I think repairs to the wallboard and the painting can be done quickly if the contractor makes it a priority. The wiring on the other hand . . ."

"What's the hang-up there?" asked Nate. "I saw the electrician leaving."

"Yeah, that was Dave Oliver. He says it may take several days, but he can't start until the fire marshal gives the go-ahead. Dave said he'd come out tomorrow with a helper if we're good to go, so we may get it done in time after all. And one really good thing just happened. I belong to the Aswontee Chamber of Commerce. The president called me a few minutes ago. He said the Chamber's going to help pay for the professional cleaning crew I hired to come help get the lodge back in shape. They'll come as soon as we've got power and water."

"Sounds like an answer to prayer," said Nate.

"Yeah, I guess it does. But I'll tell you one thing."

"What's that?"

"I'd like to have my name cleared."

■ ■ ■ ■

Nate left Rocky at the lodge and hurried home to change before driving to work. For the afternoon shift, the sheriff assigned him to the supervision of an experienced man.

"Deputy Ward Delaney," the man said, extending his hand to Nate. "You'll be riding in the car with me this week."

"Sounds good," said Nate.

While they drove, Ward explained his route. "Usually I've got a few stops I make to check up on people, mainly convicted felons. I've got a couple living in Aswontee and one out your way."

"Oh?"

"Yeah. The only one in Baxter on my list right now is Rocky Vigue."

Nate felt uncomfortable with the idea of showing up at Rocky's place in an official capacity, especially after what had happened over the last few days. He knew Rocky was beginning to depend on his friendship. But to his relief, when they knocked on the door about five o'clock, Rocky greeted them cheerfully despite their uniforms.

"Just checking up," said Ward. "How you doing, Rocky?"

"Oh, fine I guess."

"Staying out of trouble?"

"Yeah."

"Heard you met with a nasty accident the other day."

Rocky winced. "Yeah, but Nate rescued me. You should have seen him."

"I heard about it," said Ward. "Pretty exciting story."

"So, did you walk home from the lodge this afternoon?" Nate asked.

"No, Sarah and Ginnie Walsh dropped me off. Those girls are sure a barrel of laughs." Rocky's cheeks colored, and he looked away.

Nate laughed, wondering if the sisters had teased Rocky mercilessly. "Yeah, they're cute girls. I'll bet they liked Clinker, too."

"Oh, yeah, they both think he's the greatest. Hey, would you like some soda? I've got root beer and cola in the fridge." Rocky started toward the hallway.

"No, that's okay," Nate said.

Rocky's eager expression drooped. "Okay. Well, gimme a second, will ya, Nate? I've got something I want to show you."

"I wonder what this is all about," Ward said, eyeing a crack in the ceiling as they waited for Rocky to return from the kitchen.

"Beats me." Nate looked around the dingy living room. The only furnishings were a sagging couch, a floor lamp, and a small television set perched on a straight chair. Nate wondered if Rocky's parents had seen the rental, and if they would let him move home again later if he stayed out of trouble with the law.

In a moment, Rocky returned carrying a piece of worn, soiled fabric. "I didn't think to show you this before, Nate. Clinker and I took a ramble around the lake again this morning."

"Not on the ice, I hope," said Nate.

"Oh no. I kept Clinker on his leash. We followed the shore, inside the tree line. And we found this not too far from the lodge." Rocky handed the fabric to Nate.

"Those woods are probably littered with trash," said Ward.

"Yeah, but this is antique trash," said Rocky. "It's kind of cool."

Nate unfolded the fabric and shook it out. "It's a sack. Looks like something's printed on it."

"Sugar, five pounds," said Rocky. "That's not something you see in the woods every day."

Nate had to agree. He wondered how Rocky had managed to come upon the sack after all the snow that had fallen. He peered more intently at the bag and noticed another marking in dark ink that he couldn't quite make out. Below was a rusty, brown stain. "Did you dig this up, Rocky?"

"Clinker found it in the snow. He sniffed all around and came up with that."

Nate handed the sack to Ward. "Take a look."

"It's a sugar sack," said Ward. "What am I supposed to look at?"

"What's that in the center?" Nate pointed to the dark smudge. "It kind of looks like —"

"A number three," said Ward.

"Doesn't it? And that down there could be blood."

"Or not." Ward frowned at him and shrugged. "Could be mud."

Nate felt a rush of adrenaline. He had a hunch there might be something to Rocky's discovery. He leaned closer to Ward. "Jeff Lewis has been having trouble with prowlers at the hunting lodge, and now he's had an arson fire. Do you think this could be significant?"

Ward shrugged and eyed the sack again. "Well . . ." He turned to Rocky. "Do you mind if we take this with us?"

"Sure, you can have it," said Rocky. "Is it evidence? It would be cool if Clinker and I helped solve the case. Does this have something to do with the fire?"

Ward threw Nate an amused glance. "Uh, I don't know, Rocky. We'll have to wait and see."

"Let's keep this among the three of us, okay?" Nate said.

"Sure! I won't blab. And Clinker won't either."

18

A three-hour drive on Wednesday put Emily in Sainte Aurelie, Quebec. As she entered the small municipal building, a woman greeted her from her seat behind a desk.

"Bonjour."

Emily smiled. "Bonjour. I'm Emily Gray, and I spoke with you on the phone yesterday. I'm here to look for information about the Pushard family."

"Oh yes." The woman rose and walked to a bank of filing cabinets. "I did some preliminary research, and I've located some records that may help you. The local churches in the area were very good at documenting baptisms and deaths during the time you mentioned. However, nearly all of them are written in French. If you need me, I'll be happy to assist you."

Emily plunged into the pile of files the clerk had set aside for her. Within an hour, she was satisfied. The long drive and the tedious check at the border were not in vain. André Pushard had died in his hometown at the early age of thirty-eight.

"It's not what I expected to find," she admitted.

"That he died so young?" The clerk took several records they had selected to her copier.

"Partly. After all, you would think he was in the prime of his life." Emily reviewed the notes she had made. "He'd been in the lumber camps every winter for most of his adult life. He must have been a strong, healthy man."

"Yes, but the cause of death, that does not lie."

"Loss of blood."

"Yes, and this small item about a farming accident seems to confirm it." The clerk held up a dingy clipping, and Emily nodded. "Very sad."

"I can help you fill out a form if you'd like. You can send to Montreal for a copy of the official death record. But it will tell you the same thing, perhaps less than you have learned here."

"Let's do that. I'm a bit surprised that he died here. I thought maybe he died in Maine."

"No, according to this, he was at home on

the family farm for the summer when the accident occurred."

Emily completed the form and drove south to cross the border again at Jackman. As soon as she was within range of calling service, she dialed Nate's cell phone.

"Are you on duty?" was her first question.

"Yes, but I'm in the car with Ward. What's up? Are you home yet?"

"No, but I will be by suppertime. Any chance you can join me?"

"I might be able to wangle an hour for supper. I'll ask Ward."

"Great. I thought I'd cook, if you dare to risk it."

A moment later, Nate told her they would try to be in Baxter at suppertime.

"Does Ward want to come?" Emily asked.

"No, he says he's hankering for a cheeseburger plate at the Lumberjack. Meet me at my place about five thirty, okay?"

Emily smiled. "Terrific. I'll stop and pick up the groceries I'll need. If there's time, maybe we can work on the guest list tonight."

"What about the mystery? Aren't you going to tell me what you found today?"

"Not until we rough out a guest list," she insisted. "You're a champion procrastinator."

"You wound me."

She laughed. "It's true."

"All right, but I won't do any wedding preparations until you tell me everything you know about André the lumberjack-turned-villain."

"I'm not so sure he was the villain. But it's a deal."

The next day, Nate checked his uniform in the bathroom mirror before putting on his jacket. Almost time to leave for work. It had been four days since he started regular duty, but he still felt a jolt of surprise when he saw himself in uniform. He'd thought for so long that this dream would never be realized. In the last year, God had given him two things he'd despaired of ever having: a career in law enforcement and Emily. Every day he thanked the Lord.

He pulled in a deep breath and squared his shoulders. Time to meet Ward and get out there to keep northern Maine safe. He smiled at his reflection. In reality, the afternoon-into-evening shifts he'd spent with Ward so far were calm and would have bored Emily silly. They spent hours driving from one location to another, answering all sorts of calls — an auto accident, domestic disputes, thefts, traffic duty, and a harassment complaint. Because of the area's sparse population, they spent more time in the car than dealing with people. But it was the two minutes after they arrived on the scene of each call that made his pulse hammer. Anything could happen when an officer entered the picture, and they had to be prepared for the worst.

He drove to Aswontee and parked in the municipal building's parking lot. Because the officers' homes were scattered throughout the large county and they lived so far from the sheriff's office, they drove their official cars home and often met at other locations. Nate had not yet been assigned a county car, but a few minutes later, Ward arrived in a sheriff's department cruiser. Nate gathered his gear and joined the deputy.

"What do you say, Holman?" Ward asked jovially. "Ready to roll?"

"Yeah."

"No new fires or murders in Baxter, eh?"

"No, not today."

Ward drove to the edge of the main road. "Well, what do you think? Should we take a tour of your town or head toward civilization?"

"You're the boss."

Ward turned away from Baxter. "I've got

a parolee I want to check on, just to keep him on his toes. We can visit the lake later if things are slow. Oh, that folder on the back-seat has updates for you. Nothing new on the MacBriarty case, is there?"

Nate shook his head. "No, and as far as I know, the fire marshal hasn't come up with any real leads on the arson at Lakeview Lodge, either."

"The sheriff included a copy of that report in our packets," Ward said. "Pretty strange. The trouble with the electricity at the lodge wasn't caused by the fire."

"Yeah. I've thought about that." Nate scowled as he remembered the night of the fire. "We were lucky everyone got out all right. The phones and the power were out. I haven't had a chance to get out there and talk to Jeff again, but the question is, if the fire didn't interfere with the wiring, what did?"

"The report made it sound like sabotage. The fire marshal is pretty sure it was arson, and he indicated the arsonist also may have cut the power."

"Uh-huh. Well, tomorrow is Jeff's big opening, when the first guests of the season are supposed to arrive. I hope he was able to get the wiring fixed on time." Nate reached over the seat and retrieved the folder and then settled back to scan the contents while Ward drove.

"Hey, here's a report from the state crime lab on our sugar sack."

"Yeah. That brown stain was blood, all right. Human blood. That was a good call on your part, Holman."

"Do you think we should investigate where Rocky found it?"

"Yeah, we can ask him to show us where the dog dug it up."

The dispatcher called them, directing them to respond to a traffic accident on the Bangor Road. Ward turned the car around in the nearest driveway. "That's half an hour away. I guess we won't get to talk to Rocky tonight. It will probably be dark before we can get to Baxter, and we want him to show us the site in daylight."

Nate agreed and settled back in the seat. The vastness of their territory was the thing that hindered them most. People wanted a law enforcement officer instantly, but usually it took them awhile to reach the scene.

Six hours later, Ward drove at a leisurely pace toward Blue Heron Lake.

"A fender bender and a domestic. Want to grab some coffee at the Lumberjack?"

Nate shrugged. "Sure."

The dispatcher's voice came over the

radio. "PSD 9, we have a call from Lake-view Lodge in Baxter."

"Oh joy," Ward said. "The hot spot for crime these days. Take that call, will you, Holman? We can be there in ten." Ward flipped on his strobe light.

Emily stirred her cocoa. "So tomorrow you'll interview the owner of the new woodworking business, and I'll catch the Spring Carnival at the middle school in Aswontee."

"Right. Get lots of pictures." Felicia popped a cheese curl into her mouth.

"Nate's off tomorrow night, so we'll probably do something together."

"How are the wedding plans coming?"

Emily couldn't help smiling. "Terrific. Mom and I spent an hour on the phone last night. We're having the flowers done in Bangor, and they'll deliver the morning of. Hey, we need to go dress shopping."

"Plenty of time." Felicia swiveled to look at the calendar. "We've got four months, right?"

"Yeah, but I don't exactly have all the time in the world to shop for wedding gowns, and you need something really classy for your maid-of-honor dress. I did some looking online, but I think it's time I did some real-life shopping."

"Well, why don't we go to Bangor next Friday?" Felicia suggested. "That's our slowest day of the week at the paper. Unless you want to go Saturday."

"I'll see what Nate's schedule —" Emily broke off as the scanner came to life. She'd learned to recognize the dispatchers' voices and the radio codes for the state police, municipal departments, and county sheriff.

"At Lakeview Lodge, Baxter."

"Lakeview Lodge again," Felicia said.

Emily jumped up. "Nate's unit is responding." She grabbed her purse, phone, and notebook and ran for the door.

"The camera," Felicia called. "Take the digital camera." She ran over and thrust her camera bag into Emily's hands at the doorway. "Call me."

"I will."

Emily drove as fast as she dared to the hunting lodge, but the sheriff's department car had beaten her to it. The unit was parked neatly beside the porch steps. She leaped from her car and hurried in through the front door.

"Emily."

Jeff stood next to the check-in desk.

"Hi," Emily gasped. "What's going on? I heard the call on the scanner."

Jeff looked toward the staircase. "This time, I think I've caught an intruder."

"Really?" She opened her notebook.

"Yeah. Nate and the other cop went upstairs. They told me to wait here and not let anyone else up there."

"What exactly happened?"

Jeff rubbed his stubbly jaw. "Well, I was getting ready for bed, and I thought someone was in my office. It sounded like someone bumped the wall between my room and the office. None of the staff goes in there without my permission. So I went out through the sitting room, and when I got to the hallway, I saw a man wearing a ski mask come out of the office."

Emily scribbled as fast as she could.

"I was between him and the door, so he ran up the stairs."

"Wow. Is anyone else up there?"

"Yeah. Lisa, Ginnie, and Sarah. We all went out for pizza to celebrate. The girls, Sam, Lucille, and me." He gritted his teeth. "I hope they're okay. They worked so hard to help me get ready again. They wanted to party, so I took them all to the Lumberjack, even though I was exhausted. Lucille and Sam went home afterward."

"So . . . that guy is still upstairs?" Emily asked. "Do they know?"

"I called the girls right after I called the cops and told them to stay in their rooms and lock their doors. Unless he got out a window, he's still up there. See, I locked the back stairway door so he couldn't come down into the kitchen that way, and then I called the police. I went outside and kept looking around the house, and I don't think he got out. All the guest rooms on the second floor are locked, so I don't think he could get to a window. The ones on the ends of the hall don't open enough to let a man through. I'll bet he's hiding. And now the officers have him cornered."

Emily pulled in a slow, shaky breath. "How long have they been up there?"

"Maybe five minutes. They'll flush him out."

Footsteps pounded overhead, and Nate charged to the top of the main stairway.

"Jeff! When our backup gets here, send them up to the third floor."

"You've got the burglar up there?"

"He's holding Lisa hostage in the employees' lounge. Apparently he grabbed her right after you called to tell the girls he was here. Ginnie and Sarah are okay, and we're going to send them down." Nate disappeared from the landing.

Jeff stared at Emily, and she left off jotting

down the gist of what Nate had told them.

"Oh man! I shouldn't have locked him up there," Jeff said. "That was really stupid of me. He probably tried the back stairs and went up to the third floor after he realized he couldn't get out through the kitchen or the guest room windows. I should have just let him escape. Now I've put Lisa in danger again."

Emily patted his arm. "You had to make a quick decision, Jeff. You did what seemed best at the time."

A siren pierced the air.

"That's the state police." Jeff strode for the door.

As two blue-uniformed officers entered the lobby, Ginnie and Sarah Walsh hurried down the stairway, wearing their pajamas and housecoats.

"Emily!" Sarah rushed to her and threw her arms around Emily. The sisters trembled, and tears streaked down Sarah's face.

"Jeff, can Ginnie and Sarah use your sitting room?" Emily asked.

"Sure."

"Are these the hostages?" one of the state troopers asked.

Ginnie shook her head. "No. My sister and I are all right. We were already in bed, and we heard some noise in the lounge. I opened our door and saw a man in there with Lisa. She yelled to me to get back in our room and lock the door, so I did."

"We stayed in our room praying until Nate Holman came and pounded on our door a few minutes ago," Sarah said.

"Yeah, he told us he would take us to the top of the stairway and that we should come straight down here." Ginnie put her arm around Sarah. "But that guy's still got Lisa, and he's got a knife."

Jeff snatched an afghan from one of the lobby sofas and wrapped it around Sarah's shoulders. "Come on into my sitting room, girls."

"It would be better if you took them out of the building," the nearest trooper said.

"They're not dressed for it," Jeff said. "We'll stay out of your way."

"All right. But no one goes upstairs. The state police tactical team is on the way."

"How long before they get here?" Emily asked, writing furiously in her notebook.

"Two hours." The trooper followed his partner up to the second-story landing.

The Walsh sisters stared bleakly at Emily.

"Two hours?" Ginnie wailed. "It will be two hours before they can rescue Lisa?"

"I'm sure the officers who are here will do

everything they can." Emily hustled Ginnie and Sarah into the sitting room and gently probed for more details. Jeff left them for a few minutes and returned with a coffeepot and mugs.

"The coffee was already made, but I can make some cocoa if you want it, Emily."

"Don't bother. This is great, Jeff." Emily turned back to Ginnie. "So, you got a look at the burglar?"

"He had on a ski mask." Ginnie's voice shook. "But he was taller than Lisa, and he looked kind of heavy. Not fat, but . . . oh, I don't know. He was wearing a jacket, so maybe he was actually skinny. I just don't know."

"Here." Jeff placed a mug of hot coffee in her hands. "Relax, Ginnie. Emily, I think I can answer one of your questions."

"What's that?"

"The burglar's identity, of course."

"But . . ." She stared at him. "He was wearing a ski mask. I thought you didn't see his face."

"I didn't. But I saw enough to let me recognize him."

19

"Give it up," Ward said. "There's no way you can win this. Just put the knife down and let the lady go."

Nate stood on one side of the lounge doorway and Ward on the other, pistols drawn, peering in at Lisa and the intruder. The man had on a lightweight jacket and a green knit ski mask. He stood behind Lisa, one arm around her waist, and the other holding a lethal-looking knife at her throat. Lisa was shaking, and her dark eyes pleaded with them to do something.

Nate rubbed his stomach, feeling the comforting bulk of his body armor, though it wasn't designed to stop a knife. They couldn't shoot the man because of Lisa's proximity, but he and Ward could put their guns away and tackle the guy. It would be easy to take him, if not for the knife. There was a pretty good chance that if they tried it, someone would get cut up. Nate tried to keep his breathing steady and wait while Ward kept talking.

Sounds behind them drew Nate's attention. Two state troopers were mounting the stairs. Nate eased away from the doorway and motioned for them to join him at one side, down the hall.

"What have you got?" asked the first trooper, whose name tag read GRAVES.

"The owner locked the intruder upstairs, so he took a hostage," Nate said. "We don't think he has a gun, just a knife. So far he hasn't hurt anyone. Deputy Delaney has had some negotiations training, and he's trying to talk him down."

Graves nodded. "Time is on our side if he's acting rationally. We've got a state police negotiator and a tactical team on the road now."

"Good. I don't think this guy is nuts," Nate said. "I think he knew exactly what he wanted tonight."

"Which was?"

"This man or someone else has broken in here several times, but we never caught him. He wasn't going for the safe. The fact that he chose tonight is significant. It's the last night before the lodge opens for the season. By this time tomorrow, this place will be full of paying guests. Bigger chance of being seen and of someone getting hurt. He wanted to get in tonight and take his loot."

"Which was?"

Nate winced. "I'm not positive, but I have a good idea. The owner has told me about a legend where the man who built this place had a large fortune that disappeared."

"I read about that in the paper," the second trooper said. "Some vanishing treasure story."

"You mean it's real?" Graves asked.

"Maybe. Maybe not. But this guy thinks it is." Nate nodded toward the lounge. "That's what matters."

Ward stood openly in the doorway now. "Come on, stalling will only hurt your chances of getting a break. Let her go, man."

Nate eased over closer to Ward. "If it's okay by you, I'm going down to talk to Jeff Lewis and see if he's thought of anything that will help us."

"Can't hurt," Ward said.

Nate bounded down the stairway to the second floor, through the hall, and down the main staircase. Emily was halfway across the lobby.

"Nate! I was going to risk going up to tell you something."

"What?"

"Jeff knows who the burglar is."

■ ■ ■ ■

Emily, Jeff, and Nate sat at one of the dining room tables.

"That's all I can tell you," Jeff said.

"His name's Oliver, though? You're sure?"

Jeff nodded. "My first thought was that it was my brother."

"Ian?" Emily stared at him. "You actually suspected him?"

"Well, yeah." Jeff looked away. "I didn't like thinking it, but he was so bitter when he left here the last time . . . I did wonder. But when I got a good look at this guy, I could tell the body type was all wrong for Ian. This guy's a lot heavier."

"So he's the one who's been working on your wiring all winter," Nate said.

"Yeah. Ironic, isn't? I've been paying him to fix it, and he was botching it up on purpose so it would take longer. He wanted more time to look for the treasure."

"You're sure?"

Jeff bit his upper lip and nodded.

"We'll talk about this later," Nate said. "Right now I've got to take Delaney this information."

He rose and hurried into the lobby and up the stairs.

Jeff clasped his hands on the tabletop and sighed. "I just hope this is over soon and that Lisa is okay. I really care about her, you know. She's worked here for three years, and when we're busy she pitches right in and keeps things going. If one of the guests has a problem, she's right there to fix it. Everyone loves her. I just think she's terrific."

"You make a great couple," Emily said with a smile.

Jeff ducked his head. "I never really thought she'd go out with me, but this weekend, in the middle of all the craziness, we sort of clicked. She said she'd love to go out with me after we get the lodge put back together and get past opening weekend. But now, I've locked a homicidal maniac upstairs with her. How stupid was that?"

Emily reached over and squeezed his hand. "Take it easy. God is in control up there. You'll have a chance to tell Lisa how much you appreciate her."

Jeff's eyebrows drew together. "Let's hope so."

"David Oliver."

The burglar glared at Ward Delaney over Lisa's head. Nate held his pistol ready in case the burglar made a sudden move.

"Come on, Dave, we know who you are," Ward said. "You might as well take the mask off. I can tell you're sweating. Take it off and talk to me."

The masked man tightened his hold on Lisa, and she winced as the knife blade made contact with the skin below her chin.

Ward lowered his voice to a confidential purr. "Dave, you've spent months working on this place. Probably since you did the first estimate on the wiring for Jeff Lewis last fall. You planned how you could spend extra time here and look for the money. You dragged your feet on the wiring job. When that wasn't enough, you broke in. You even started a fire to give you an excuse to do more work. You disconnected a few crucial wires in case the fire didn't do the job. Presto. Lewis had to call you again."

The burglar's arm relaxed. Slowly he lowered the knife a few inches. "One night without anyone bothering me — that's all I needed. I figured if I made a lot of smoke, Lewis and his people would move out for a few days at least. But after the fire, the cops were here all night. And Lewis moved back in the next day. Can you beat that? Smoke and all, he came back. I had to keep sneaking in."

"What I can't figure out is why you spent

so much effort on this cockamamy treasure story," Ward said. "If there was a treasure here, it's been gone for a long time."

"That's all you know."

"Oh yeah? Let Miss Cookson go, Dave. We'll talk about it."

"I never meant to hurt anyone."

"I know you didn't," Ward said soothingly. "Give yourself a chance here. Let the girl go, and we'll have a chat. You can tell me all about it."

Oliver stood unmoving for a long moment. Nate could see Lisa's lips tremble as she tried not to move.

The knife clattered to the floor. The burglar reached up and pulled the knit mask from his head. Lisa plunged forward, and Ward stepped aside to let her pass.

Nate pulled her quickly to one side of the doorway as Ward filled it again with his broad form.

"Come on, Lisa," Nate said. "Let's get you downstairs. Did he hurt you?"

"My arm's a little sore, but I'm okay. Thank you!"

Behind them, Nate heard movement and the unmistakable sound of handcuffs closing. Ward Delaney's voice came loud and clear. "You have the right to remain silent . . ."

■ ■ ■ ■

Emily stood at the bottom of the main staircase, staring up at the landing above. She could hear voices, but she couldn't see anyone.

Lord, keep Lisa safe. Help them to get this guy without anyone being hurt.

Steps sounded in the upstairs hall, and Nate and Lisa appeared at the top of the steps.

"Jeff," Emily called.

Jeff hurried out of his office. "Lisa!" He ran to meet her as she got to the bottom of the stairs and wrapped his arms around her. "I'm so sorry! Can you forgive me?"

"It's okay," Lisa whispered, patting his back. "I'm all right, and everything's going to be okay."

Emily looked up at Nate, who had stopped halfway down the staircase. "Everything okay?"

He nodded.

"I love you," she mouthed.

Nate winked and turned back toward the landing.

Detective Blakeney arrived just after Graves called the dispatcher to cancel the tactical team's response. Ward Delaney and Nate were placing their prisoner in the back of their cruiser.

"Guess I missed the fireworks," Blakeney said with a nod to Delaney.

"All over but the shouting," Ward agreed as he closed the car door on Oliver.

Blakeney eyed Nate for a moment. "How'd your rookie do?"

"Good." Ward slapped Nate on the shoulder. "He knew the victims, and his knowledge of what happened here previously helped us put this thing together."

"Glad to hear it." Blakeney's gaze drifted toward the lodge porch, where Emily and Jeff stood, and landed on Emily for a moment. "I see the press is well represented."

She went down the steps and extended her hand to him with a smile. "Nice to see you again, Detective Blakeney."

He shook her hand briefly and turned back to the two deputies. "So, you're transporting the prisoner to the county jail?"

"That's right. You can come along if you want. He's already told us enough to link him to the arson fire here last week, and we're hoping to tie him to several other crimes."

"I hear you. If you think he was mixed up in the MacBriarty murder, I want to hear what he has to say."

Ward nodded. "Come on down to Bangor, then. We'll be booking him."

"Right. But the hostages are fine?"

Nate said, "Yes, sir. They're staff here at the lodge, and they've gone up to their rooms on the third floor. If you want to speak to them, I can call them down."

"No, that's all right," Blakeney said. "So far, it's your case. Do you think this is the same guy who broke in last fall?"

"Yes, sir. He's admitted that."

Blakeney walked closer to their cruiser and eyed Nate through narrowed eyes. "I don't get it. What was he looking for?"

Nate smiled and held out a worn, yellowed sheet of paper enclosed in a plastic bag. "He had this in his pocket."

Blakeney took the bag and squinted at the paper in the dim light from the bulb over the porch. "What is it? I can hardly read it. I see a number five there and a three here. It looks like a floor plan."

"It is. A floor plan of this lodge." Nate stepped closer to Blakeney and pointed to various spots on the crude treasure map. "Those numbers designate locations in the framework of the building, mostly between walls and under floors. I believe this plan was made over a hundred years ago."

Blakeney blinked at him. "Oh, yeah? Where's it been all this time? The bozo you caught tonight hasn't been carrying it around for a century."

Nate glanced around at Jeff. "Why don't you explain it to him?"

Jeff shook his head as he came down the steps. "No, you're doing great. Every time I open my mouth around the detective, I get in trouble." He flashed a contrite look at Blakeney. "No offense."

"All right. The short version." Nate pointed to the old paper once more. "Ward found this in David Oliver's pocket when he patted him down. The prisoner was upset when Ward took it from him. I recognized it as a drawing of this building. He told us he first found it last fall when he came to do the estimate for Jeff. See, the lodge had only minimal wiring for a long time, but Jeff was having everything done over with new wiring and plumbing, and he wanted lots of new outlets and overhead lights added. Oliver had to poke around and see where he could access the different locations for electrical fixtures so he could do what Jeff wanted without tearing up too many walls. Upstairs, they added ten bathrooms and tore out some walls and added new ones, so putting in new wiring wasn't so much of a problem up there. They could put it in the new walls. But downstairs Jeff wanted to keep the antique feeling and preserve things like the woodwork in the library."

"So the electrician had to be more careful on the first floor?"

"Yes, and he examined crawl spaces and gaps between walls that hadn't been looked into for years."

"And he just happened to find a treasure map."

"Well, it wasn't that simple." Nate looked over at Jeff, and his friend nodded.

"My family looked for this treasure all my life, but we never found anything, so we concluded it was just a story." Jeff inhaled deeply. "It's incredible that he actually found something we'd missed all that time."

Nate nodded toward the old paper. "Oliver said this was in a cubbyhole in the wall of the laundry area, behind the kitchen."

"That area used to be part of the owner's private quarters," Jeff said. "There was a small opening in the wall between the library and what's now the laundry room. I showed it to Oliver last fall, thinking it would help the workmen who did wiring and insulating."

"That's right," Nate said. "That part of the lodge was never wired in the old days. A few outlets for the laundry had been added on the wall between it and the hallway, but the old wall between the laundry and the library hadn't been tampered with. When Oliver got in there to see if he could run wiring without destroying the paneling and the antique woodwork, he pulled off a couple of short boards that were nailed to the studs inside the wall to see if he could run some wires through there. Jeff and his siblings had never thought to remove those boards. And Oliver saw the edge of a piece of paper tucked behind a stud. He got it out, and this is what he found."

Blakeney shook his head. "I still don't believe it has to do with the old man's money. Oh, I remember reading the story a few months ago." He scowled at Emily. "It probably stirred things up. This guy might not have broken in or started that fire —"

"Or killed Mac MacBriarty?" Emily asked. Her blue eyes searched Blakeney's face. "Trust me, Detective, I've thought of that."

Jeff straightened his shoulders. "Mac? No, Emily, don't blame yourself for that. We don't know that David Oliver had anything to do with Mac's death."

Blakeney turned to Delaney. "Did you ask him about the murder?"

"Not yet, but we will. You can count on that."

"Even if he did it," Jeff said, "it wouldn't be your fault, Emily. I told Oliver about the treasure myself, before you even wrote your story. He was curious about the lodge's history. He came poking around here because of what I told him and finding that map, not because of your story. He was hoping to find some evidence that the treasure was real."

"Correction," Nate said. "He was here tonight hoping to find more money. I think he already found the first installment. According to that map, there were five locations in the lodge where something significant could be found. Oliver found one of them at some point before the fire last week. Maybe on the night Ian and Phoebe and their families were here."

Emily gasped. "That thumping I heard in the night."

"Or maybe he'd found it while he was working here over the winter and was looking for the rest when you heard him last week." Nate looked expectantly at Ward. "Remember the sugar sack Rocky Vigue found?"

"Number three," Ward said. "You think it came out of this lodge?"

"I do," Nate said. "Look at the diagram. We can check, but I think the number five on the paper corresponds to the outer wall in the guest room next to Emily's. If Oliver was poking around in there the night we and Jeff's family stayed at the lodge, Emily would have heard him for sure."

She frowned. "We should check the baseboards and under the rugs in that room."

"Yes, we should," Nate agreed. "It's possible Oliver decided to go after that cache next."

"If what you're thinking is true, there must be at least one stash left that's hidden so well he couldn't find it easily while he was doing the wiring," Jeff said. "He didn't want to give it up, so he kept coming back to look for it, even after his work was done."

"But that sack." Emily's brow wrinkled in a frown. "Nate, you think he found some money in an old sack last winter and got away with it?"

"That would explain Clinker finding the sack in the woods. That would be the first one, I'm guessing. But he could have found another one that night you heard the thumping."

"But the sack Vigue found had been out in the woods a while," Ward said.

Nate turned toward him. "Yeah, we really

need to have Rocky show us the spot where he found it. I'm thinking maybe Oliver found it last winter, got out of the lodge quickly — maybe someone scared him off — and stopped out in the woods to examine the contents of the bag . . ."

"Say he transferred the money to his pockets or a duffel bag," Ward said.

Nate nodded. "He left the sack in the woods, whether intentionally or by accident, I don't know, but Rocky and his dog found it."

Ward beamed on the detective. "And do you know something else, Detective Blakeney?"

"I give up. What?"

Ward grinned at Blakeney. "We sent that sugar sack to the state crime lab last week. And they found human blood on it."

20

Nate, Ward Delaney, Emily, and Jeff gathered in the lodge's lobby late the next morning. Emily's pride in Nate swelled as she watched him. He'd always been kind, smart, and great-looking. His uniform gave him an air of confidence and authority that suited him well.

My future husband. She sat back in an armchair, content to let him and Ward have the spotlight.

"Well, Lewis, looks like you're off the hook," Ward said, smiling at Jeff. "David Oliver has confessed to several breaking and entering incidents and the arson. He admitted the pocketknife you found last fall was his. And we've got him cold on kidnapping Lisa Cookson."

"But not killing Mac?" Jeff asked.

"Not yet," Nate said.

"He's not talking on that one," Ward admitted.

Nate shrugged. "Don't lose heart, Jeff. We're still putting the evidence together. If we can prove Oliver stole the bags of money from the lodge . . ."

"You found an old sack in the woods," said Jeff.

"But we can't prove it held money, or that it came from this building."

"We didn't actually see it in Oliver's possession," Ward added, "and we won't get fingerprints off the fabric. But we might find a lot more evidence. And if we can connect him to the MacBriarty murder, the state's mobile crime lab will be back here so fast it will make your head spin."

"What can we do?" Jeff asked.

"For starters, we can look for the rest of the money," Nate said. "We can try to find any sacks Oliver missed. Remember, if he'd found them all, he wouldn't have come back last night."

Ward opened a folder he had brought and handed each of them a sheet of paper. "We checked the drawing out of the evidence locker this morning and made enlarged copies of it."

Jeff peered closely at the diagram in his hand. "If you're right, Nate, these stashes can't just be stuck between the walls. We would have found them a long time ago, or

Oliver would have stumbled on them all when he was stringing the wiring. They must actually be hidden behind the structural members, or else boarded up inside the walls like the map was."

"One way to find out," Nate said.

Emily felt a rush of excitement. She jumped to her feet. "Count me in!"

"What, you want to go treasure hunting right now?" Jeff asked.

"With your permission," Nate said. "Don't you wonder if the rest of the money is really there?"

"Someone else could have found a sack sometime within the last hundred years and just quietly walked off with it," Emily said. "We need to check all the places marked on the drawing."

"Well, I hate to wreck anything that's just been fixed . . ." Jeff shrugged and guffawed. "Why not? We won't sleep tonight if we don't try. I'll get some tools."

Lucille came out through the doorway that led to the dining room. "Would you like coffee for you and your guests, Jeff?"

"Not now, Lucille. But I was thinking . . ." Jeff turned to Ward Delaney. "Would you mind if I let Lisa and the Walsh sisters in on this? Our first guests won't arrive until after lunch, and I think they've earned the right to see this thing through to the end."

"Well, we don't want them to touch any-thing," Ward said.

"Lisa could have been killed last night," Emily reminded him.

Ward shrugged. "All right. But if we turn up any evidence, you civilians have to keep back and let us handle it."

"Absolutely." She grinned up at Nate, and he stooped and kissed her lightly, as though he'd caught her excitement.

"Come on, kids," Jeff said. "This is seri-ous business. Lucille, would you mind ask-ing the girls if they want to join us?"

Lucille bustled away toward the kitchen, and Jeff pored over his sheet. "I'm pretty sure some of these spots are accessible from crawl spaces, though why Ian and I never found them beats me."

"Do you think Mr. Eberhardt made this map?" Emily asked.

"Him or the person who stole the money from him."

Nate nodded. "It had to be someone in the lumber camp the night Eberhardt died. Somebody either killed him or found him dead —"

"And we may never know which," Emily said. "My opinion is that Eberhardt would have left the money in the safe. Someone else — and I'm banking on André Pushard — either killed him or discovered that he had died of natural causes and took advantage of the opportunity."

"Right. That person took the money and hid it in the lodge, planning to retrieve it later. He made himself a map showing where he left it all." Nate puzzled over the intricacy of the plan. "I expect he divided it up so that even if one part was found, the others would still be hidden until he could get them."

"Why didn't he take the map with him when he left?" Wade asked.

Jeff looked up. "That's a big question. We know the other men suspected André, the man who drove Eberhardt to town and back, of making off with the money. I think he hid it and made the map. But why did he leave the map here when he went home to Quebec?"

"Yeah," Emily said. "I did some research at the state archives a few months ago, and I found an old journal kept by one of Eberhardt's clerks. It's written in French, but I photocopied it and brought the pages home. I've found the name Pushard in it in several places. I've been meaning to have it translated, but I've been so busy, I haven't gotten around to it. But tomorrow I'm meeting with the French teacher at Aswontee High. I'm hoping to get some answers."

"Pushard left here and never came back," Nate said. "That makes him seem a probable suspect to me. The person who hid that money was prevented from ever retrieving it."

"Right." Emily sat down hard on her chair and stared off toward the window.

"What are you thinking, Em?" Nate asked.

"I was thinking about the death record I found in St. Aurelie. André went home to Quebec to spend the summer on his family's farm. He died in a farm accident that year — the summer after Eberhardt died and the money disappeared."

"Hey! Maybe he planned to just leave it here over the summer and let the talk die down," Jeff said. "Then when he came back the next winter to work as usual, he could retrieve it when he had the opportunity."

They all looked at each other.

"To me, that makes more sense than Mr. Eberhardt taking the money out of the safe and hiding it that night," Emily said. "It would have taken hours to hide the sacks so well. I just can't imagine the old man doing that."

"If we don't find anything to the contrary, it will make a nice speculative ending to your story," Jeff said.

"You mean you'd let me print another installment in the *Journal?*"

"How could I say no?"

She grinned. "All right, let's get on it."

Lisa, Sarah, and Ginnie burst through the kitchen door, with Lucille close behind them.

"Is it true you're going to look for the treasure?" Lisa asked.

"Yes, we are," Jeff said. "But the deputies are in charge, and we're just spectators."

"Got it," Lisa said, and the other women nodded.

"Well, Mr. Lewis, which of these numbers on the floor plan looks easiest to find, in your opinion?" Ward asked.

Jeff tapped his copy of the map. "Number one. There's a small door in my bedroom wall that opens on a crawl space between the bedroom and office walls. I don't think I could fit in there anymore, but I was in it plenty of times when I was a kid. And Emily might be able to squeeze in there now."

They hurried to Jeff's bedroom. Jeff opened the small white door situated low in the wall, and Nate handed Emily his flashlight.

"Careful, Em."

"I will be." She turned the beam into the

dark cranny and crawled inside. Six feet along between the walls, the space seemed to hit a dead end. However, a closer inspection showed an even narrower space around a corner, toward the outside wall. She leaned forward as far as she could, with her head against a two-by-four in the wall. She wondered if David Oliver had managed to squeeze into the small tunnel. Though he wasn't as tall as Jeff or Nate, he was heavier.

"Hey, guys!" Her voice sounded tiny in the enclosed space.

She wondered if they heard her, but Nate called, "What is it?"

"Looks like someone ripped off a couple of boards here." She reached into the crevice and gingerly pulled out some scraps of wood and a bent nail. She hated to put her hand into the small niche between the walls. Brown recluse spiders, here I come! The cavity seemed to be empty.

She picked up the scraps of wood and the nail then backed slowly out of the crawl space. When she emerged into Jeff's room, she stood and handed the wood to Nate.

"I found those in there around a corner. It's a tight fit, and I could barely reach in, but there's a gap in the wall. It looks like it was boarded up and someone ripped it open." She held out the nail. "See this? The bottom part of it's shiny."

The men leaned closer.

"That's been worked recently," Ward said.

Jeff looked at the nail closely. "So Oliver was in there looking for money."

"There's none there now." Emily frowned. "If there was any, where is it?"

"Maybe that was the sack Rocky Vigue found," Jeff said.

Nate shook his head. "No. That one was number three. This should be number one."

Emily sighed. "Maybe we were wrong about the numbers. Maybe they aren't sacks of money at all."

"Or maybe Oliver found this number one sack on a different occasion," Ward said.

Nate's features brightened. "You could be right. If he found the first sack last fall, or even the night Mac was killed, that would give him the incentive to keep coming back to look for the rest."

"Could be he's found them all." Jeff dropped onto the edge of his bed. "He might have found it all and made off with it. In which case, we may never see it."

"Then he wouldn't have come back last night," Emily said. "Don't give up hope, Jeff. Where's number two?"

They all looked at their diagrams.

"Looks like it could be under the service

stairway, but I've looked there before."

"In the wall beside it?" Nate asked.

Ward perked up at the thought. "Or maybe one of the stairs has a cache under it."

Jeff shook his head doubtfully. "You can see up under the steps from below. None of them is boxed in. I'd hate to tear out the whole staircase for nothing."

"Maybe we'll find something else if we're all looking together," Sarah said. Jeff stood and led them into the hall and to the doorway near the kitchen, where the back stairs came down.

"Oh yeah, I didn't unlock this last night after you caught Oliver." He took a key ring from his pocket.

While they waited for him to unlock the stairway door, Emily slipped her hand into Nate's. He squeezed it and smiled down at her.

"What —" Jeff stood holding the edge of the door and staring into the stairwell.

After a moment, Ward cleared his throat. "What is it, Lewis?"

Jeff moved aside so they could see inside. On the bottom step lay an old cotton sack with a faded green and yellow design printed on it. A dark slash of ink marred the center of the pattern.

Emily let out a little squeal. "Number one!"

Nate whistled.

"Oliver must have had it on him last night when you chased him up the stairs, Jeff." He picked the sack up carefully. "Where can I open this?"

"Use my worktable," said Lucille.

They all followed her into the kitchen. Lucille hurried to spread a clean towel over her work surface. "There. Put it right there."

Nate rested the sack on the table and gently worked at the string that held the open end together. The knot was small, and he looked up in frustration. "Emily, your hands are smaller than mine. See if you can get this. Careful, now."

Emily reached out and deftly worked the string until the knot loosened. She stood back and let Nate remove it from the neck of the sack. Nate peered inside and smiled.

"Well, Jeff, I'd say this is part of your treasure."

Gently he eased the old banknotes from the sack. Several bundles were held together with paper bands. Jeff whistled. "Do you need to take it to the county sheriff's office?"

"We should enter it as evidence," Ward said. "But we'll give you a receipt, and you'll

300

get it back soon. We can even count it in your presence if you'd like."

"Thanks." Jeff stared at the money and let out a low chuckle. "After all this time."

"Let me get a picture." Emily raised her digital camera and snapped a photo. "And don't forget, Jeff, there should be more."

"What if he got the rest?"

Ward scratched his chin. "We can check to see if anyone's turned in a large amount of old money recently at one of the banks. Of course, this loot is in silver certificates. It may be worth more than the face value."

"Yeah, we should check with coin dealers, too," Nate said. "It would be hard to get rid of a large amount of old money without drawing attention."

"Well, we're getting a warrant to search Oliver's house," Ward said. "We should have it before the end of the day. If he found some money before and has it stashed in his house, we'll find it."

"This should be enough to get us permission to check all his accounts, too," Nate said. "If he's made a large deposit since last fall that doesn't correspond to payment received for work he's done, then we'll try to trace it back and see if he sold or turned in a batch of old bills."

Jeff nodded. "Well, I guess I'm ready to

tear into that back staircase."

"Let's think about this." Emily held up her copy of the floor plan. "The money had to be hidden without the other men seeing it done. If André had been sawing and hammering in the night, someone up in the barracks would have heard him."

"But he made sure the hiding places were well concealed," Ginnie said.

"Right. But I don't think he did anything upstairs where the old bunks were or ripped up an entire staircase." Emily held up her map. "See how the number 2 is off to the side of the stairway on the plan?"

Nate consulted his own drawing and let Lucille look at it, too. "Yeah. Right beside the top step. Maybe there was a loose floorboard up there."

"Wouldn't my grandfather have found it?" Jeff asked.

"Maybe. Is the original flooring still in the hall above?"

"It's hardwood," Emily said quickly.

Jeff drew in a deep breath. "You're right. The hallway on the second floor is all oak. I don't think it was that nice when the lumber camp operated. I'll bet my grandfather laid that oak floor when he converted it to a hunting lodge in the 1930s."

"So maybe he laid the new flooring right

over the old one, using the original boards as a subfloor," Nate said. "If he didn't find the second sack at that time, it would be effectively sealed up for the next seventy-five years or so."

"What if Mr. Lewis did find it?" Lisa asked.

Jeff shook his head. "We'd have heard about it. Grandpa couldn't keep a secret like that. And he'd have probably taken the place apart piece by piece looking for more."

"Well, do you want to take up some floorboards?" Ward asked.

"Would André have done that while the men were sleeping?" Nate said, and everyone looked at him.

Jeff hesitated. "Probably not. And I do think Grandpa would have found it if it were in the floor up there." They stood in silence for a moment, then he said, "We've got sack number one here, and we know Oliver found sack number three."

"Right," Nate said.

"Do you think we could wait on looking for the others? Oh, not long. Just a few days."

"Because your guests are arriving today?" Emily asked.

"Not just that." Jeff looked around at them sheepishly. "I just kind of feel as though I'd like Ian and Phoebe to be here when we look."

Emily's face fell.

"Do you want Emily to delay publishing her story in the paper?" Nate asked.

"I gave my first piece to Felicia this morning," Emily said. "It will come out in tomorrow's edition, telling how Nate and Deputy Delaney caught David Oliver, and about his taking Lisa hostage. It's gone to the printer, Jeff. I'm afraid it's too late to stop it."

"That's all right," Jeff said. "But if we could just keep people from knowing about the money. I don't want our guests ripping into walls or anything. And I think Ian and Phoebe would come back for that. Even though we'll have guests here, we ought to be able to have a private family celebration in my quarters and look for the other three caches while the guests are out fishing."

Nate thumped him on the back. "I think that's a great idea."

Jeff smiled at them all. "This weekend's going to be really busy. But if I ask them to come . . . oh, say, Tuesday, can you all be here?"

"We'll be here, anyway," Ginnie said, looking at her sister.

Nate grinned. "I wouldn't miss it for the world, and I know Emily wouldn't, either."

Jeff looked at Lisa. "How about you?"

"Sure. I'd be honored."

"Great." Jeff looked at his watch. "We'd better get busy now. Our first guests should arrive any minute."

21

Rocky trudged ahead of Nate and Ward through the woods, swinging the end of his scarf around in the air.

"Right about here, I think." He stopped in a low spot near a group of small pines. "Yep, that's where Clinker and I found the sack."

Ward nodded. "Thanks, Rocky."

"You're welcome." He grinned and shoved his hands in his pockets.

Nate surveyed the area. Most of the snow had melted, though a little still lingered under the trees, and the ground was spongy. "Doesn't look like we'll find anything else here."

"Nope," said Ward. "But we'd better make a thorough search, in case Oliver dropped something else. Then we'll go over to his place."

They started at the spot where Clinker had discovered the sack and carefully examined the ground around it.

"What's that?" Nate asked, pointing to the muddy ground.

Ward pulled tweezers from a pocket and used them to lift a soggy, muddy strip of discolored, thick paper.

"Dunno."

Nate peered at it and shrugged. "Let's keep it." He held out a small evidence bag, and Wade dropped it inside. Nate scribbled on the label the location and time of discovery.

They spent another half hour surveying the area but found nothing else. They said good-bye to Rocky and returned to their vehicle. When they arrived at the electrician's house, they began to methodically search together. An initial sweep for a safe proved fruitless, so they began going over everything in the living room.

Finding no sign of the stolen money, they went on to the kitchen. Nate searched the stove — in the oven and the drawer under it, and under the burners — while Ward went through cabinets. Nate made his way around the edge of the room to the refrigerator. When he opened the freezer, he caught his breath.

"Hey, Ward! I think I've got something."

Ward came over and looked inside. "Not

a normal place to keep luggage."

"My thoughts exactly." Nate pulled out an old duffel bag and laid it on the kitchen table. He unzipped it and revealed several bundles of money.

"Well, it seems pretty clear-cut now," said Ward. He took a bundle of bills from the bag and flipped through them. "Old silver certificates. But there's only about ten grand here. I wonder if there was more. That sack Lewis found yesterday on the stairs had almost thirty thousand."

"Guess we'd better keep looking. Hey." Nate reached out one finger and touched the paper band around the bundle of money. "Look familiar?"

"Yeah. That's what we found in the woods this morning. Oliver emptied the sack there and put the money in this duffel bag to bring it home."

A thorough search of the rest of the house yielded nothing.

"What now?" Nate asked. "Where would you stow a large sum of money?"

"In the bank," Ward said automatically. "If I could convince the teller I came by this stuff legally. I saw a bank statement in Oliver's desk a minute ago, and the warrant covers his bank accounts. Let's go."

"We'd better take his business records,

too," Nate pointed out. "He would have some legitimate large deposits from pay received for electrical jobs."

At the bank, one of the tellers on duty remembered serving someone who brought in five thousand dollars in silver certificates a few months earlier.

"Do you remember who it was?" Ward asked.

"No, but I remember that he said his grandmother died and the cash was found in her house. So we cashed them in, and he deposited the money in his account."

"At face value?" Nate asked.

"Yes, we don't give added value for antique money. That's for dealers."

Nate nodded and slid a copy of Oliver's last bank statement toward her. "Could you please bring up David Oliver's account?"

"Sure," said the teller.

"We need to know what deposits he's made since November."

The bank's records revealed that Oliver had deposited nearly twenty thousand dollars a few months earlier that couldn't be accounted for from his business.

"Okay, I'd say that likely takes care of at least one stash," said Ward. "The question is, did he find any more?"

"We didn't find records for any other bank

accounts," Nate said. "We could try calling coin dealers. Oliver might have gone to one of them so the bank wouldn't start asking questions."

"Good idea," said Ward.

Nate made a few calls, and one coin dealer in Bangor said he'd been asked about the market for silver certificates but that none were brought into his shop.

"Do you think we should go to the shop and question him?" Nate asked Ward.

"I don't think so at this point. We know Oliver made off with one bag of money — the number three sack that Rocky recovered. He put the bulk of it in the bank, probably spent some, and kept the rest in his freezer while he tried to decide what to do with it."

Nate's cell phone rang, and he answered it.

"Holman, this is Bill Garner at the state crime lab. I have some news for you."

Nate listened and felt his pulse accelerate. "Wow. This sheds a bit of light on things."

"What's up?" Ward asked as Nate put his phone away.

"Looks like the state police will be taking over from here. The lab has matched the blood on the sugar sack to Mac MacBriarty."

■ ■ ■ ■

Nate burst into the *Baxter Journal* office
where Emily and Felicia worked. "Big news,
Em!" he called. "Want to come over to the
lodge with me?"

Emily jumped up from her desk. "Absolutely!"

Felicia cleared her throat loudly.

"You're not busy, are you?" Nate asked,
eyeing Felicia.

"She's not busy," said Felicia. "She's only
got a paper to put out. But never mind, I'll
let her go on official capacity." She laughed.
"You'd better bring a story back for me,
Emily."

Emily shot Felicia a mischievous smile.
"I'm sure I will. Thanks, Felicia." She and
Nate started out the door. "Is this about the
murder?" she asked him.

"Yep. I want to wait and tell you when
we're with Jeff, if that's okay."

At the lodge, Jeff welcomed them inside.
Nate had called ahead to say he and Emily
were coming and they had good news.

"What's the story?" Jeff asked, leading
them into his sitting room.

Nate couldn't help laughing. "You're in
the clear. Oliver's confessed to killing Mac."

"You're kidding," said Jeff.

Nate clapped him on the back. "It's all over, buddy."

"Wow, I don't know what to say." Jeff's eyes threatened tears.

"So, what happened?" Emily asked eagerly.

Nate sat on the sofa. "Sit, sit."

Emily sat beside Nate, and Jeff collapsed into an armchair, still smiling incredulously.

"The state police questioned Oliver extensively, and under the weight of the evidence, he confessed to finding sack number three in the attic wall. Mac apparently caught him with it and confronted him in the third-floor hallway as he was sneaking out of the lodge."

"And that's when he killed him?" asked Emily, eyes wide.

"Yeah, Oliver stabbed him right there in the hallway. He dumped Mac in his bed, locked the door, and sneaked out. But he'd gotten blood on the sugar sack —"

"So he had to ditch the sack," finished Emily.

"Right," said Nate. "In case someone found it in his possession. That would be pretty incriminating. But thanks to Rocky and Clinker, the sack was found near the lodge, and we sent it in to the crime lab."

"He's in jail now, right?" Jeff asked.

"Oh yeah. He's charged with murder, theft, arson, kidnapping, and terrorizing. He's at the Penobscot County Jail in Bangor until his arraignment. Apparently the judge already denied him bail, so he's got to stay put until the trial. He's not going anywhere for a long time."

"Good place for him." Emily shivered. "I can't believe that guy was sneaking around here for months."

"Me either," said Jeff. "To think he might have killed any of us, too, if we'd caught him at his game."

"God protected us," said Nate. "That's for certain."

The next week, Jeff invited Nate and Emily to join him at the lodge with Ian, Phoebe, and their families.

"It's sort of a celebration," Jeff explained to Nate on the phone. "And I know you and Emily want to be in on the treasure hunt."

"We'd love it!" said Nate.

"Could you also invite Deputy Delaney to come?"

"I'm sure he'd like to be there and see the end of this story," Nate agreed.

At noon on Tuesday, they all gathered at the lodge. Emily watched as Phoebe, Kent, and Ian entered.

Ian stopped in the doorway and looked back outside. "You kids stay out there for a few minutes. And don't run off. We may not be here long." He shut the door.

Jeff stepped forward. "Thanks for coming."

Phoebe eyed him critically. "I don't know why we did. Suppose you enlighten us."

Jeff looked away for a moment then faced her. "Look, Phoebe, I want to apologize for upsetting you the last time you were here. You, too, Ian and Kent. I didn't intend to insult you or make you feel bad."

Phoebe inhaled through her nose and said nothing.

Ian shrugged. "Hey, bro, no hard feelings. And we heard about the fire you had a week or two ago. Tough luck, man."

"Thanks. It was a setback, but we were able to open on schedule."

Kent cleared his throat, "Listen, Jeff, in my opinion, you didn't do anything wrong when we were here. If anyone should —"

"Is this it?" Phoebe snapped. "Do you have anything else you want to tell me? Because it would have cost a lot less to grovel over the phone."

Emily edged closer to Nate, wishing they had let Jeff confront his siblings alone. Nate squeezed her hand.

Jeff winced. "No, Phebes. That's not all. Something good has happened, and I wanted you and Ian and Kent here to celebrate with me."

"They caught the murderer," Ian said. "We heard."

Kent nodded. "Yeah, that's great. So that's all taken care of. Case solved."

"But you don't know why he killed Mac MacBriarty," Jeff said. "You don't know why the man who was rewiring this lodge stabbed my best guide in the hallway upstairs."

After a moment's silence, Ian said, "Okay, I'll bite. Why did he?"

Jeff smiled. "Remember the treasure?"

"Well, yeah." Ian smiled slowly. "You don't mean that dirtbag was looking for the treasure?"

"Yes. He has been for months, ever since I had him come give me an estimate last fall. He may even have been in the house the last time you were here. Remember Emily said she heard someone in one of the empty rooms that night?"

Phoebe fixed her gaze on Emily, and Emily wished she could shrink and hide. "So there was a real, live intruder that night? Imagine it."

"And it gets better," Nate said. "Wait until

Jeff tells you what we've found out in the last few days."

Jeff grinned. "Yeah. What I really wanted you here for was to help me look for the rest of Eberhardt's treasure."

"The rest of it?" Phoebe asked.

"That's right. The burglar found two sacks of money in this building. But there are supposed to be three more. I was sort of hoping you all and the kids would help me look for them."

Ian smiled. "If that doesn't beat all. The treasure is real!"

Kent nodded at Jeff. "Decent of you to invite us."

Phoebe licked her lips. "Yeah. Okay. I guess."

Over Lucille's lunch of corn chowder and buttermilk biscuits, they discussed the results of the case and speculated about the location of the remaining three stashes of silver certificates.

"We've got copies of the map," said Jeff. "I've been studying it, and I'm hoping it won't take us too long to find the money once we start searching. I want you all to help me find the money. That is, if you want to."

"I'm all for it," said Ian. The children all

chimed in with enthusiastic assent.

"Here's what I don't get," said Phoebe. "Why did the guy hide the money in the walls? Why didn't he take it and run?"

"The men wouldn't have let him go," said Emily. All eyes turned toward her. Nate saw her face flush from the attention.

"I did a little research," she explained. "As I told some of you last week, I got hold of an old diary kept by Alexander Eberhardt's clerk, and recently someone was able to translate it for me. Apparently the other men in the camp suspected André Pushard of stealing the money after he found the boss dead. Some of them even suggested he might have killed Eberhardt, but the boss's body showed no signs of foul play."

"They knew André had the money, then?" asked Phoebe.

"They thought he did, anyway," Emily went on. "According to the journal, the other men harassed him. They even searched his belongings."

Jeff's eyes lit up. "So he hid the map to make sure they wouldn't find it on him."

Emily nodded. "That's what I think, too. They wouldn't leave him alone, and he got angry and left the camp. André probably hid the money sacks in the lodge the night Eberhardt died, but he couldn't retrieve them with everyone watching him. So he left, hoping to return later to recover the loot, after talk had died down. But he died before he could do it."

Everyone was quiet for a moment. At last Jeff pushed back his chair and reached for a folder on the next table. "I've got four copies of the map here. I figure we'll all look for the stash near the back stairs first, and then we'll divide into teams. Ian and his family, Phoebe and hers, Emily and Nate, and me and Ward. We'll also take Lisa, Ginnie, and Sarah along. Those are the staff members who were here the night the murderer was captured. You can search anywhere except guest rooms that are occupied, as soon as the guests have left for their outings. But please don't rip up any boards without me."

Nate laughed. "Not unless you offer to pay for the repairs."

"That's right," said Jeff.

They all trooped to the back stairs near the kitchen.

"Any ideas?" Ward asked. "It would be a shame to tear all the stairs out, as you pointed out before."

"Well, we wondered if it could be under the flooring above the stairs, but I've changed my mind about that. That would have been right in the barracks where the men slept back then. André couldn't have lifted any floorboards and nailed them back in place without waking them all. I'm not so sure he could have done much messing with the staircase, either."

"I just thought of something," Emily said, and everyone turned to look at her. "I don't think the man who kept that old journal liked André much. Before Mr. Eberhardt's death, he mentioned a couple of times that he was sure André had been drinking. But they never saw him with a bottle or anything. What if André had made these hiding places earlier. Before he had a chance to steal the money?"

"You mean . . ." Nate smiled slowly. "To hide his whiskey bottles?"

"Something like that." Emily shrugged. "If he had been hiding stuff for a long time, anyway, he'd have known right where to put the money that night, where no one would find it right away." She looked at the back stairway.

"The third step's always been creaky," said Phoebe. "We always skipped it when we were sneaking into the kitchen for cookies."

"That's true," said Jeff. "Although I never sneaked around." He winked at the kids.

They all laughed.

"Sure, Uncle Jeff," said Chelsea. "Like I believe that."

Jeff knelt on the floor at the bottom of the stairs and ran his hands over the third step. "I still don't think it can be under the stair step. You can look right up underneath, where we store boxes."

"Why don't we take up that one step?" said Nate. "We might find a clue."

"I'll get some tools," Ian offered.

"Yeah, go ahead," said Jeff. "One step can't hurt much. If there's nothing under there, we can rethink this."

When Ian returned with a pry bar, everyone waited with bated breath as Jeff carefully lifted the step, doing as little damage as possible.

"I don't know." Jeff and Ian leaned close, while the others waited above and below them on the stairs. "I don't see anything."

Phoebe sighed. "Too good to be true."

"Wait a sec," said Ian. He touched the wall at the side of the steps, just below where the tread had been. This wall has been patched."

"Think so?" Jeff frowned. "I guess we'll have to tear out some plaster to be sure. And it's that old horsehair plaster."

"We can do it without making a big mess," Ian assured him. "And I'll patch it up afterward. I just Sheetrocked my den. I'll do a good job."

Jeff laughed. "What's a little more plaster dust around here, after all the remodeling we've done?"

Ian took the crowbar and began to pound and dig at the sloppy patch in the wall. When he had a hole big enough to stick his hand through, Ward passed him a flashlight.

"Well, there's something in there all right."

"You'd better put gloves on," Phoebe said.

"Yeah, maybe it's a mouse trap with a dead mouse in it," Chelsea chortled.

"Ha, ha." Ian dug at the plaster and enlarged the hole. He looked at Jeff. "You want to do the honors?"

"No, go ahead," Jeff said.

Ian shone the flashlight's beam into the hole and grinned. "It's here!" He reached in and carefully pulled out a dusty sack. He passed it to his brother.

Jeff held it up so they all could see. "Number two. Three down, two to go." He passed the sugar sack back to Ian, who loosened the drawstring and reached inside.

"Wow!" said Will. "How much money is in there, Dad?"

"Count it," said Ian, handing the cash to his son.

Will sat down on the bottom step and

started to count the money with Chelsea and Derek looking on greedily.

"And it's worth more than face value," said Emily.

"Yes," Ward said. "The coin dealer told us this morning that those old bills are worth a lot, and especially certain years."

"So handle them carefully, kids," said Kent, who had remained in the doorway at the bottom of the stairway.

Phoebe shook her head. "To think we went up and down these stairs a million times and never thought to look underneath."

"Hey, we were kids," said Jeff. "We thought lost treasure would be buried outside or sewed inside a mattress."

Emily grinned. "And if André had a hole in the wall under the step already, so he could stick a whisky bottle in there, he could easily shove in a bag of money and then come back later with enough plaster to close the hole."

"Where are the other two spots?" Nate asked, scrutinizing his and Emily's copy of the map. "Looks like one in the lobby and one on the second floor."

"That must be near the room I stayed in," said Emily.

"Let's get that one," said Nate.

Emily nodded.

"I kept room 6 vacant on purpose today," Jeff said. "Here's the key. You won't disturb any guests if you go in there."

"I guess the rest of us will ransack the lobby then," said Ward. He looked at the map in his hand. "It looks to me like it's near the fireplace."

Nate and Emily headed upstairs to the guest room where Oliver had been prowling around months earlier.

"It must be on the outside wall," said Emily. "Can I see the map?"

Nate held the map out so they could both study it. "It's hard to tell where on the wall, because these rooms weren't divided this way back then. But we know it can't be in the new, interior walls."

"It looks to me like it's marked near the window," said Emily. "That makes sense, because Jeff said this was a big, open barracks in the old days. But the window frames are the original woodwork."

"Maybe we should have brought that pry bar." He touched her arm, and she looked up at him. "If this was part of the barracks, it was like a big dormitory room."

"I think so."

"Then how could he hide something here? We sort of agreed before that he couldn't hide anything on the second story, or someone else would have seen him."

Emily frowned. "Good point. But this is a corner room. Maybe it was walled off back then, too."

"Like for a supervisor or something?"

She snapped her fingers. "That French journal. It said André was the foreman for this camp. I'll bet he had private sleeping quarters. And he might have had another secret hiding place in his own room." She crossed the room to the window. "Years ago, I heard about a woman who bought an old farmhouse, and while she was redoing one of the bedrooms, she found a diamond broach hidden under one of the window-sills."

"Sounds like a good place to hide something," said Nate. "Maybe we should wait until Jeff's ready to take a look."

"Hey, I think we've got something down here!" Ward called from below. "You two want to come see?"

"Oh, let's go down," said Emily. "I don't want to miss it."

In the lobby, the others were all staring up at the side of the fireplace.

"That one rock's loose," said Jeff. He pointed with the broomstick he was holding. "I kind of wiggled it a little with this, but we need someone to pull it out. Chelsea didn't want to be hoisted up."

"You got a stepladder?" Nate asked Jeff.

"You can boost me up," said Emily. "I'd love to do it."

"Be my guest," said Jeff.

Nate and Ward hoisted Emily up high enough so she could reach the top of the fireplace.

"This one?" She reached for the rock Ward had indicated and tried to wiggle it. It moved just a tiny bit. "Well . . . it's a tight fit, but maybe . . ."

Lisa called, "Hey, we've got the ladder." She and Ginnie came from the hallway that led to the kitchen and laundry, carrying a stepladder between them.

Nate and Ward lowered Emily to the floor, and Jeff opened the ladder and positioned it for her.

"I think a knife would help, if anyone has one," Emily said.

Kent produced a pocketknife and handed it to her. She climbed the ladder and began to pry at the mortar around the stone. After a bit of coaxing, it came out in her hand. She handed it down to Nate, exchanging the rock for Ward's flashlight.

She peered into the hole. "I can't see anything. And I don't think one of those sugar sacks would fit in there."

"Too bad," said Jeff as she backed down the ladder. "It seemed like a perfect spot."

"There's another patching project for me," Ian said with a chuckle.

"Are any of the other rocks loose?" Nate asked.

"I'm not sure," said Jeff. "We've checked all the stones within reach. That's why I went for the broomstick." He climbed two steps on the ladder and started tapping and prodding at the other stones around the top of the fireplace.

"Did you two find anything upstairs?" Ward asked.

"Not yet," said Emily. "But we think we know where to look."

"I think this one's loose," said Jeff, tapping a reddish brown stone with the end of the broomstick. "But maybe I'm getting frustrated so I'm imagining things."

"I saw it move, too, Uncle Jeff," said Will.

"Can I get this one?" Derek pleaded. "I'm small for my age."

Phoebe laughed. "That's the first time I've heard you boast about being small."

"Derek's turn," said Jeff. He climbed down the ladder and let Derek take his place.

Ian passed him his knife. "Now, be careful."

"Oh, boy, this one's coming out," Derek cried gleefully. "Here she comes." He fumbled as he pulled the rock out, and it clattered down the front of the fireplace. Nate caught it as it glanced off the mantel.

"Good save. Anything in there?" Ian asked eagerly.

"Patience, patience," said Derek. "Drumroll, please." He reached into the hole and felt around. At last he pulled something out.

Jeff and Ward steadied Derek as he climbed down. He raised the sugar sack in the air and cried, "I'm rich, I'm rich!"

"Good work," said Jeff. "Thanks."

"My pleasure." Derek grinned. "Although I do charge a small commission fee."

Phoebe elbowed her son in the ribs.

Jeff tousled his hair. "That just leaves the one upstairs. Emily, did you say you know where to look?"

"We think it might be under the windowsill," she replied. "I've heard of people hiding things there before, and the mark on the map looks right for that."

"That means we'll have to pry the boards up." Jeff wrinkled his forehead.

"For that kind of money, it's worth it," said Phoebe. "You could buy Home Depot with what you've found."

Jeff laughed. "Not quite. Well, let's see if Emily's right. Someone got that pry bar?"

"I have it," said Ian.

Jeff gathered a few more tools, and they headed upstairs.

Emily pointed to the number 5 on the map. "I think it has to be near the window, based on this."

"I'll go along with that," said Jeff.

"Wait a sec." Nate stepped forward and laid his hand on the windowsill. "Emily has a theory that André may have had this corner as his private quarters, since he was a foreman. I know this wall has been redone, but the original woodwork is still here." He ran his hand slowly over the sill and along the trim board beneath it.

"We've stained that wood," Jeff said.

"I know. Did you open up the wall?" Nate asked.

"No. Grandpa had added the pine paneling way back when."

"Hold on." Nate felt a slight indentation in the bottom of the trim board. He exerted more pressure, and the board lifted out, away from the wall below the window. A narrow opening was revealed, only three inches deep, beneath the window sill.

Emily went to her knees and shined the

beam of Nate's flashlight into the crevice. She laughed.

"What?" Jeff asked.

"André's stash, all right." She pulled out a flat, squarish, half-full bottle and handed it to Nate. "And . . . tada!" Reaching in again, she carefully slid out another cloth sack. "Here you go, Jeff. The final installment."

"Not so much in this one." Jeff untied the string and looked inside the sack. "Plenty, though." He looked around at all the eager faces. "Let's go down to the library and get comfortable."

The staff members thanked Jeff and went back to work, but the family gathered in the cozy old library with Emily, Nate, and Ward. Jeff set the three sacks of money on the library table. He cleared his throat and looked solemnly at his siblings. "Ian, Phoebe, I've decided to give each of you one-third of the money."

Ian's jaw dropped. "You're kidding, right?"

"Oh, Jeff . . ." Phoebe stopped and shook her head. Tears glistened in her eyes.

"I want to share the treasure with you," Jeff went on, "because I love you, and I think God would want me to."

Nate smiled at his friend. It was good to hear him sound so happy again.

Jeff said, "I talked to the president of the bank in Aswontee, where I have my accounts. They'll keep this money safe for us in their vault until the rest is returned from the state police. Then I'll have it appraised and sold. I'll have your shares transferred to your accounts."

"Woohoo!" Derek cried. "We're rich!"

"Hey, Dad, let's talk about my allowance," said Will.

"Now can I get a laptop?" Chelsea begged.

"I'll discuss it with your mother," said Ian. "And remember, it could be weeks, or even months before the processing is done."

"It shouldn't be long before you get back the bills that were entered as evidence," Ward said. "They'll photograph them all and check for Oliver's fingerprints, but they shouldn't have to keep it. If they do find his prints on it, they may keep a few representative bills until his trial."

"Sounds good," said Jeff.

Phoebe looked at her younger brother. "I don't know what to say, Jeff. You don't have to divide the money."

"I want to."

She clamped her lips together and looked down at the floor. After a moment, she looked up at him. "I'm sorry I made a fuss when we were here before. I really thought you were . . . Oh, what does it matter what I thought? I was wrong. Can you forgive me?"

Jeff stood and went over to her chair. "Of course, Phebes. I love you." He bent down to hug her.

"Thank you," she said. "And now I think we should see about fixing the things we tore up."

Jeff smiled. "Thanks. I'll put Ian in charge of that. There's some leftover plaster and mortar mix in the utility room."

"Come on, kids." Ian winked at Jeff. "Thanks, bro." He herded the family out of the library.

"Say, Phoebe," Jeff called. "Would you mind asking Lisa to come in here?"

"Sure, no problem."

"That was a really nice thing to do," Emily said softly when all of Jeff's family had left the room.

"Well, it only seemed right," said Jeff.

A moment later there was a soft tap on the library door, and Lisa entered. She smiled at Nate and Emily. "Hi. Jeff, you wanted to see me?"

"I wanted to give you this." Jeff handed her an envelope. "I suppose it's really poor compensation for what you went through . . ."

Lisa stared at him, her face flushing. "You don't have to give me anything."

"Well, what am I going to do with all this money we've found? I wanted to share it." He smiled at her. "Please take this. It's a check for five thousand dollars. I know it won't erase the memories of the fire, or the burglar holding his knife on you, but . . . well, I hope it will make it a little less traumatic to remember."

She lifted her hand then let it fall to her side again. "Really, Jeff, I don't want it. The only thing I needed that night was coming down the stairs when it was over and finding you waiting for me. And you know what? I'd kind of hate to have something like this between us. Money, I mean." Her face flushed a becoming rose, but she looked up into Jeff's green eyes.

He stepped toward her and slipped his arm around her. "Lisa, if that guy had hurt you . . ." He smiled and squeezed her. "Well, maybe we'll talk about this later." He turned and looked at Nate and Emily. "And I have to thank you two. You've been really supportive and helpful."

"I hope you're not thinking of unloading more of your money on us," said Nate.

"We don't need anything," said Emily. "Just your friendship is enough."

"I thought you'd say that. So, I decided to give you an engagement present." He handed an envelope to Emily.

Nate leaned in to watch her open it.

Emily pulled out a card. Inside there was a voucher for two weeks per year at the lodge, all expenses paid. "For life, or as long as Jeff owns the lodge," Emily said. "Thanks, Jeff. This is great."

"You're more than welcome," said Jeff. Nate noted that Jeff's hand found Lisa's, and her flush deepened, as did her smile.

That evening, Nate and Emily stood on the dock at the marina watching the sunset.

"I'm so glad to see the ice melting." Emily sighed softly, snuggling in closer to Nate. Within a week or two, she should be able to move out to her cottage on the island.

"Me, too," said Nate. "Sometimes it seems like winter lasts forever around here. I'm so glad this was the last one I'll spend without a wife."

Emily laughed. "Just four months now. It's getting close."

"Yes it is," said Nate. He bent his head to kiss her. "It sure is."

ABOUT THE AUTHORS

Susan Page Davis is the author of ten historical novels, two children's novels, and six romantic suspense books, in addition to cozy mysteries. She and her husband, Jim, live in beautiful Maine, where he is a news editor. Both are active in a small, independent Baptist church. Their six children range in age from 13 to 30. When possible they enjoy spending time with their five far-flung grandchildren. Susan has home-schooled all six children. She enjoys reading, needlework, genealogy, and meeting her readers. Visit her Web site at: www.susan pagedavis.com.

Megan Elaine Davis grew up in rural Maine, where she was homeschooled with her five siblings. She holds a bachelor of arts degree in creative writing from Bob Jones University and has published poetry, articles, and humorous anecdotes in various publications. Besides writing, she enjoys reading, traveling, theater, cooking, and chatting with friends. Her favorite authors are Agatha Christie, Jane Austen, and C. S. Lewis. *Treasure at Blue Heron Lake* is her second novel. She will soon become Mrs. John-Mark Cullen and make her home in England.

You may correspond with these authors by writing:
Susan Page Davis and/or Megan Elaine Davis
Author Relations
PO Box 721
Uhrichsville, OH 44683